"What is it that you want of me?"

Lucille composed herself to take the plunge. "I want what you offered me on the phone."

"And what was that? Please remind me…"

"A strictly sexual and very private affair," she bit out.

"Ah, yes," he drawled. "I do recall. I'm to be your secret lover and you, my secret playmate. So for how long would you envisage this…arrangement…lasting?"

Forever, came the involuntary thought.

Dear Reader,

I admit it! I find playboys fascinating. I love reading about their glamorous lives, their beautiful women, their many affairs. There's something exciting about these wicked devils who dare to do what an ordinary man wouldn't—or couldn't.

I've always thought a playboy makes an excellent romantic hero, because he is the ultimate challenge. Can one special woman make an often cynical man reassess his lifestyle and yearn for something finer, deeper and more permanent?

When my editor asked me to write a trilogy, I happily chose playboys for my heroes. Three handsome Aussie males who seem to have it all but find, once they meet that one special woman, that they want *her*…her respect, her love. Only this time getting what they want isn't so easy as it usually is.

I hope you enjoy AUSTRALIAN PLAYBOYS. Do write to Harlequin Presents® and let us know what you think—and which heroes personally appeal to you!

Miranda Lee

Miranda Lee

THE PLAYBOY IN PURSUIT

The Australian
Playboys

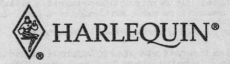

HARLEQUIN®

TORONTO • NEW YORK • LONDON
AMSTERDAM • PARIS • SYDNEY • HAMBURG
STOCKHOLM • ATHENS • TOKYO • MILAN • MADRID
PRAGUE • WARSAW • BUDAPEST • AUCKLAND

ISBN 0-373-12140-7

THE PLAYBOY IN PURSUIT

First North American Publication 2000.

Copyright © 2000 by Miranda Lee.

This edition published by arrangement with Harlequin Books S.A.

® and TM are trademarks of the publisher. Trademarks indicated with
® are registered in the United States Patent and Trademark Office, the
Canadian Trade Marks Office and in other countries.

Visit us at www.eHarlequin.com

Printed in U.S.A.

CHAPTER ONE

'LUCILLE, when *are* you going to start dating again?' Michele asked between sips of her cappuccino.

Oh-oh, Lucille thought ruefully. Here we go again.

'Surely you don't mean to stay single and celibate for the rest of your life,' Michele swept on, 'just because you had one bad marriage. I don't doubt your Roger was a right royal pig, but not all men are like that. Take my darling Tyler, for instance...'

'No, thanks,' Lucille said with a dry laugh, then downed the last delicious mouthful of jam and cream doughnut. 'He's all yours.'

Michele plonked her coffee cup down with an exasperated sigh. 'When are you going to believe that Tyler really loves me? That he's really changed? That his playboy days are well and truly over?'

Lucille was tempted to say in thirty years or so. But that would have been too cruel. Michele was only three weeks back from her honeymoon and still glowing. Lucille didn't have the heart to destroy her best friend's romantic illusions about her handsome new husband.

But, truly, what chance did that marriage have of going the distance? Sure, Tyler seemed to be madly in love with Lucille at the moment. But would he feel the same in six months' time, when the heat of the honeymoon cooled down and old habits kicked in?

The son and heir to the Garrison media fortune had

a long history of throw-away girlfriends and Lucille had no faith in a wedding ring changing that. She'd warned her friend at the outset not to fall in love with such a man, just to have an affair and enjoy the sex—which was reportedly fantastic—without getting emotionally involved.

But of course that had been futile advice with someone like Michele. The girl was too nice for her own good. Heck, she'd stayed loving and loyal to her first boyfriend for ten years. And *he'd* been a total rat. What chance had Michele's sweet heart had against the golden boy of Sydney's social set, once he'd set his sights on her?

Yes, Michele's marriage was doomed, in Lucille's opinion. But she wasn't about to say so. She regretted not being clever enough so far at pretending to believe it was a case of true love all round.

'Don't take any notice of me,' Lucille said swiftly. 'I'm just an old cynic. If anyone could make a man change it would be you.' Michele might be twenty-eight-years old, and a brilliant advertising executive to boot, but underneath the brunette's surface sophistication snuggled a soft, sweet soul. Life hadn't made her hard, or cynical, as it had Lucille.

Maybe that was why Lucille enjoyed the other girl's company so much. Because, for a while, she could soak in the warmth of her sweetness, rather like a lizard basking in sunshine.

She missed Michele no longer living in the flat next to her. She hated seeing the 'For Sale' sign out at the front of the building. Now she was really living alone, with no other close friends, just nodding acquaintances. Thank God their respective workplaces were both in North Sydney, so they could have regular lunches together, plus the odd shopping expedition.

Still, their friendship would never be quite the same now that Michele was married.

'Don't think you can avoid answering my first question.' Michele resumed determinedly. 'You're only thirty years old, Lucille. And, might I say, one stunning-looking woman. I want to know when you're going to get over Roger and move on with your life.'

Lucille might have resented any other person saying such things to her. But she knew Michele meant well and wasn't just being a busybody.

'I *am* over Roger,' Lucille replied, coolly wiping her sugared lips with a serviette. 'And I *have* moved on with my life. I have a challenging and satisfying career, a nice place to live, which is wonderfully close to my office, and a great girlfriend I can bitch to when I feel like it. I'd date if I wanted to. But the truth is, Michele, I'm just not interested in the opposite sex any more. I'm quite happy being single and celibate.'

'What a load of old rubbish! You are *not* happy being single and celibate. You're lonely as hell. And you *are* interested in the opposite sex. Women who aren't don't dress like you do. Just take a look at the outfit you're wearing today.'

Lucille's eyes blinked with surprise, then dropped to her favourite cream woollen suit. 'This old thing? You have to be kidding. Okay, so the skirt's on the short side, but the jacket's thigh-length and not at all tight. I'd hardly call it a provocative outfit. My boobs are well hidden. I consider this suit on the conservative side of my wardrobe, actually.' As opposed to the seriously sexy clothes she'd bought when she'd first left Roger and had gone through her wildly defiant stage.

Back then, she'd been determined to go out and paint Sydney red, but she had found when men made passes at her she just went cold all over.

'Your boobs might be well hidden but your legs sure aren't,' Michele argued back. 'And your legs are just as provocative, attached as they are today to five-inch heels. Haven't you noticed the looks you've been getting from the male passers-by?'

They were sitting at an outdoor café on the main street in North Sydney, whose central business district was beginning to rival Sydney's city centre across the bridge. Streams of office workers were always on the move at this hour, more than half of them male.

Lucille was used to male attention—the type that tall, voluptuous green-eyed blondes invariably got—so she really hadn't noticed. Neither did she care.

'Let them look,' she said coldly. 'Because that's all they'll ever get to do. Look.'

'Lord, Lucille, what on earth happened in that marriage of yours to make you so bitter and twisted?'

Lucille stiffened, then shrugged. 'I could never explain it in a million years. You have to live some things to understand them.'

Michele looked alarmed. 'Your husband didn't... *abuse* you, did he?'

'Abuse me?' Lucille considered that concept for a few moments. She'd never thought of her ex's behaviour as abuse before. But of course that was exactly what it had been. Emotional abuse. That was why it had taken her so long to crawl out from under it. She'd been a type of battered wife for years, with all its accompanying loss of self-esteem and confidence.

But that was in the past now. Lucille saw no point in dragging it up for continual analysis. Her marriage to Roger was best forgotten.

'No, of course not,' she told her worried-looking friend. 'He was just a low-down, cheating scumbag, okay?'

'Okay. Look, I'm sorry I brought him up. I know you hate talking about him. And I'm sorry I nagged you about dating again. I just want you to be happy.'

'Happiness doesn't always come in the shape of a man, Michele,' Lucille pointed out.

'Agreed. But misery doesn't always come in the shape of a man, either. It all depends on the man in question. And I don't believe you've given up all hope in that regard. You yourself described your dream man to me one day a few months ago. If I recall rightly, aside from him being tall, dark and handsome, you said he'd have hot blood running through his veins, not cold beer. He'd genuinely like women and always put you first, even before his mates and his golf and his car.'

Lucille laughed. 'Did I say that? I must have been day-dreaming. Such a species of male doesn't exist. Not in Australia, anyway.'

'Yes, he does. I married one.'

'Tyler's tall, *fair* and handsome.'

'Don't split hairs. I'm sure there are some fantastic dark-haired blokes around. But who knows? Maybe your dream man won't be from Australia. You deal with a lot of foreign men in your job, don't you?'

'Well…yes…'

Lucille worked for an agency which specialised in handling the needs of corporate executives transferred to Sydney from overseas. Her title was that of Relocation Consultant.

As for the men she met in the course of her work...

If Lucille had been in the market for dating—or affairs—there were plenty of applicants. Not a week went by when some man didn't hit on her. The fact that the majority of these men were married didn't exactly reduce her cynicism about the male sex and their capabilities regarding faithfulness.

Still, best she not mention that little fact to Michele at this moment, either.

'Unfortunately, Michele,' she explained, 'most of the foreign men I handle are family men. They come complete with wives and children. That's why we're in business. International companies finally realised that shifting husbands and fathers around the globe willy-nilly with no help was causing premature resignations. You don't want me dating a married man, do you?'

'Of course not. But surely *some* of these corporate execs must be single. Or at least divorced.'

'True. Some are. And quite a few have already tried to chat me up, believe me,' she confessed. 'Several have even been very good-looking.'

'And?'

'No spark.'

'Never?'

'Never.'

'I find that hard to believe, Lucille. You're saying you're *never* attracted to a man?'

Lucille decided a little blunt honesty was called for

here, or Michele was never going to let this subject drop. 'I used to think after I left Roger that I'd have no trouble having an affair, just for the sex. I like sex. Or I used to, once upon a time. But not even the most handsome, charming man turns me on any more. That part of me has died, Michele. My marriage killed it.'

'I don't believe that. Not for a moment. You've just been terribly hurt, that's all. Your libido will come good one day, Lucille. Your divorce only came through last year, for pity's sake. It's just a matter of time.'

Privately, Lucille didn't think she had enough time left in her life for that miracle to happen.

'Meanwhile, dating doesn't have to lead to sex,' Michele swept on blithely. 'What's the harm in just going out with a guy every now and then? You don't have to go to bed with him if you don't want to.'

'I assure you I definitely won't want to.'

'Fair enough. So stop looking for that spark before you say yes. The next time a nice guy asks you out, just go. Who knows? Maybe your hormones are just out of practice. They might fire up once you put yourself in the right environment. Nothing like a candlelit dinner to put a girl in the mood.'

Lucille smiled a wry smile. 'You're such an optimist. And a born romantic.'

'I know you think that, but I'm not really. I'm actually a down-to-earth realist.' Michele put down her empty coffee cup. 'I'm also snowed under at work, so I'll have to love you and leave you shortly. I only have this week to complete the campaign outline for Femme Fatale's new line of perfumes. Did I tell you about that?'

'No. What about it?'

'Remember the girl my boss brought to my wedding?'

Lucille nodded. Who could have forgotten the striking creature on Harry Wilde's arm that day? Cropped black hair. Big violet eyes. Seriously sexy dress.

'Her name's Tanya,' Michele was saying. 'Anyway, *she* was the mystery heiress who inherited Femme Fatale. You know? The sexy lingerie company? You don't know?' Michele asked when Lucille looked blank.

'I've heard of Femme Fatale, but I know nothing of any mystery heiress.'

'I thought I told you. Amazing story. It goes like this. The previous lady owner was killed in a car accident and left her controlling interest in the company to her nearest female relative, who just happened to be Tanya. Anyway, she was the girl Harry wanted the beauty salon for a while back. Remember, I asked you if you knew of a place where you go in a bag lady and come out a supermodel?'

Lucille did remember. She'd recommended Janine's, a local and very expensive beauty salon where a woman could indulge herself in every treatment known to mankind. She'd treated herself to a day there after her divorce papers had come through, and continued to use their services on a regular basis. A girl had to have *some* vices, other than a penchant for doughnuts.

'Some bag lady *she* turned out to be,' Lucille said drily. 'That girl was supermodel material from the word go.'

'Well, I did warn you that Harry wouldn't be seen dead with a real bag lady.'

What playboy did? Lucille thought caustically.

'Anyway, apparently she'd been brought up in the bush and didn't have too many clues on how to dress and present herself. Harry had her made over and *voilà!*'

'Good enough for advertising's Superman-about-town to take to bed, I presume,' came Lucille's tart comment.

'It's more than just sex. Neither of them have said anything yet, but Tanya's sporting an enormous sapphire ring on her engagement finger. I've also seen Harry with her, and he's not the Harry of old. He's different. Gentler. Kinder.'

'Another playboy changing his spots, Michele?'

Michele shot Lucille what supposedly passed as a killer look. But the girl didn't have a real killer look in her repertoire. Lucille, however, could freeze a person at ten paces if needs be.

Chastened that she'd provoked her friend into even a semblance of fury, Lucille muttered, 'Sorry,' and dropped her far too expressive green gaze into the last dregs of coffee in her own cup.

'And so you should be,' Michele chided. 'That cynicism of yours is going to get you into trouble one day, Lucille. What is it with you and playboys, anyway? From the little you've said, I gather your ex was just an ordinary Aussie guy. What have you got against men like Tyler and Harry? Why do you hate them so much?'

Lucille blinked. Hate? She didn't hate them. She just didn't trust them, with their too handsome faces,

their flash cars and their corrupting bank balances.
Having their way in life was as natural to them as
breathing. Women fell for them in droves, invariably
compromising their own moral standards and allowing
themselves to be shamelessly used, either as temporary
girlfriends or trophy wives.

This always struck a nerve with Lucille, perhaps
because she hated the thought of any woman being
used. She wasn't sure if Tyler was consciously using
Michele, but it worried her that he might be.

She could hardly say that.

'I don't hate Tyler,' she said carefully. And, really,
she didn't. He was a very charming, very likeable
man. 'I...I just think it's difficult for men like him to
settle down to being husbands and fathers, that's all.
You're my best friend, Michele. I want you to be
happy.'

Michele's face softened. 'But I *am* happy. As for
Tyler settling down... Please don't worry about that.
He's a wonderful husband and he's going to make a
wonderful father. You know, Lucille, beneath the
hype, playboys are just ordinary people, like you and
me. They have hearts and feelings. They can fall in
love. And they *can* change. Love changes them.'

'Yes, yes, I'm sure you're right. I'll try to keep a
more open mind in future.' Not to mention a shut
mouth! 'And I promise to consider saying yes to the
next suitable candidate who asks me out.' Consider,
then dismiss. Lucille felt confident there wasn't man
on this planet who could tempt her to go out with him,
no matter how tall, dark and handsome he was.

'Humph! You're just saying that.' Michele swept up
her handbag from where it had been lying at her feet

and stood up. 'I have no doubt that, come Christmas, you'll still be manless.'

'Well, Christmas *is* only a couple of months away. Attractive, single foreign men don't come along every day of the week, you know.'

'I guess not. Oh, well, I tried. See you.'

'I'll give you a call if one shows up,' Lucille called after her.

Michele grinned back over her shoulder. 'You'd better, or you're dead, girl.'

Lucille watched her friend hurry off down the street, the picture of confidence and happiness. Her head was held high, her stride jaunty, her shoulder-length brown hair blowing out breezily behind her.

Hard not to concede that marriage to Tyler Garrison suited her.

Or was it the sex?

Lucille stood up abruptly from the table. She wasn't going to think about marriage, or sex. Or anything which made her feel down. She'd come a long way with recovering her self-esteem and she wasn't about to start falling back into old patterns of feeling badly about all the years she'd wasted on Roger, or worrying about the fact she'd ended up frigid.

Who knew? Maybe Michele was right. Maybe her hormones were only sleeping. Maybe one day a man would walk into her life and change how she felt, both about the opposite sex and her own apparently lost libido.

Meanwhile, Lucille wasn't going to hold her breath waiting for that to happen. She headed back towards her office with her own head held high, her stiletto heels clacking boldly on the pavement, her long honey-blonde hair blowing back from her exquisitely made-up face.

This time she did notice the male heads swivelling round for a second glance as she walked by. But this time her reaction to their ogling was pure satisfaction.

Not that Michele was right. She didn't dress for men. She dressed for herself. To feel good. And to project the person she now was.

Not Mrs Roger Swanson, downtrodden doormat, but Lucille Jordan, a mature woman with a mind of her own, confident in her single status, her career and her person. And if her sexuality was in limbo, no way was she going to say so by dressing like some shy little mouse. She wanted her appearance to shout to the world that she was a success as a woman in every sense of the word.

Okay, so it was a lie. But the world was full of lies. And liars.

If you can't beat 'em, join 'em.

That was the name of the game these days for Lucille.

Survival.

CHAPTER TWO

LUCILLE's workplace was above a florist's shop in a narrow side street. It had a steep, thigh-firming staircase leading up to a small reception area, behind which squatted four cubicle-style offices, none designed to impress.

No need, really. The staff at Move Smooth usually met their clients at the airport, or in hotel lobbies. Advance business was always done over the telephone, or by fax. They had an excellent word-of-mouth reputation and prided themselves on their personal as well as their professional touch. All the consultants were women, trained by the boss to soothe clients' frayed nerves in five minutes flat, as well as anticipate problems before they popped up.

The boss was Erica Palmer, an ex-corporate wife in her late forties who'd experienced first-hand what was required in the relocation business. A strawberry blonde, Erica was attractive rather than beautiful, with a whip-thin figure, hard blue eyes and a reputation for ruthlessness. She'd started up Move Smooth several years earlier with the small fortune settled on her during her divorce, and now supervised her successful little moneyspinner from her multimillion-dollar harbourside home.

Lucille was her newest employee, poached from one of the real estate agencies Move Smooth regularly used. When Erica had offered her a job Lucille had jumped at the chance, having tired of the dog-eat-dog attitude which abounded in property sales. She wasn't earning any less money and her job made her feel good at the end of most days.

There was nothing like the relieved smile and sincere thanks of a harassed wife's face when she discovered that you'd found her just the right place to live, placed her children in good schools, stocked the cupboards and fridge with enough food to survive for a few days of jet lag, and provided the addresses and telephone numbers of everything she could possibly need, from doctors and dentists to video stores and all the local takeaways.

Move Smooth's company motto was, 'Attention to detail and perfection in all things.'

Which was another reason why Lucille dressed well. Her boss demanded it.

Not that Erica would ever have suggested the five-inch heels Lucille was wearing that day. Not really practical, considering the running around associated with the job. But Lucille didn't have any appointments that Monday, so what did it matter? She liked wearing high heels and never donned any lower than three inches. It was partly a rebellious gesture, born from being told always to wear flatties because she was above average height and 'men don't like girls to be taller than them'.

Or so her mother had drummed into her when Lucille had started to date.

Lucille no longer felt inclined to follow any of her mother's many maxims on feminine behaviour. With her divorce from 'dear Roger', she'd become a failure in her mother's eyes, and nothing would ever change that. Her father hadn't been too impressed, either. 'What in God's name do you want in a man?' he'd asked, scowling at her.

Lucille had learned to live with both her parents' disappointment and criticism by rarely going home, despite the Jordans living only a few miles away in the leafy Sydney suburb of Thornleigh.

Lucille struggled up the steep staircase in her extra-high heels, deciding that perhaps such shoes were best kept for trips to the theatre after all.

'You're to ring Mrs Palmer straight away,' their receptionist told her as soon she reached the top landing. 'She said it was an emergency.'

Lucille hurried to her cubicle, reaching for the phone as she sank gratefully into her chair.

Erica answered on the second ring.

'Lucille, Erica. Jody said there was an emergency.'

'You can say that again. I have a volcanic Val Seymour in my lounge-room, pacing up and down like he's Mount Etna on the smoulder, insisting I find him some place to rent for the next four months, starting this very night. Apparently he's had a massive falling out with his father and refuses to even consider attempting a reconciliation. I did suggest he stay here with me for a few days till things calmed down, but you know Val.'

'Actually, no,' Lucille commented wryly, 'I don't. Know Val, that is. Though I do know who you mean.' Hard not to when he and his father's affairs graced the tabloids and women's magazines with regular monotony.

Val Seymour was the illegitimate son of Max Seymour, legendary showbiz entrepreneur and the biggest womaniser since Errol Flynn. Max owned the harbourside mansion next to Erica's and they had a long-standing friendship, which was probably sexual judging from the familiar way they acted together. Although sixtyish, Max was still a good-looking man, with piercing blue eyes, steel-grey hair, solid muscles and bottomless bank accounts. In short, he still had what was pretty irresistible to a lot of women.

Not irresistible to Lucille, however, who'd met Max a couple of times at Erica's monthly parties and had found his suave aren't-I-wonderful? attitude left her even colder than usual.

Val Seymour was a chip off the old block, from what Lucille had heard. Though she'd never met the man. He spent a lot of time overseas. She'd read the scandalous stories, however, and seen pictures in the papers.

Thirtyish, and handsome as the devil, he wasn't in his father's physical mould, having taken after his Brazilian mother, inheriting her dark hair, dark eyes and lean dancer's body. His sexual behaviour, however, was pure Max; each man was touted always to have a fling with the leading lady in whatever show he was currently producing. Max Seymour was reputed to have bedded most of the world's top female singers, dancers, skaters and stage actresses. According to the gossip rags, Val Seymour wasn't far behind.

Of course, when the show stopped, so did the affair.

But there was always another show, and another dazzlingly beautiful and talented bedmate.

Only yesterday there'd been an article in a Sunday news supplement about the Latin American dance spectacular that Seymour Productions was bringing to Sydney's Casino for the coming summer holiday season. There had been pictures of the show's beautiful and flamboyant lead dancer standing between her two backers, her flashing black eyes turned flirtatiously up towards the son while the father's arm had been wrapped possessively around the girl's slender waist.

Her name was Flame. No surname. Just Flame.

No doubt not her real name. Still, as a stage name, it said it all. The advertisements for the show—which was called *Takes Two to Tango*—claimed that Flame's dancing was hot enough to scorch the stage.

Lucille wondered if the falling out of father and son might have had something to do with competing for the fiery Flame's favours. If Lucille was any judge of the behaviour of a bruised male ego, then it looked as if the father had won.

'What kind of place is Mr Seymour Junior looking for?' she asked Erica.

'Something close to the Casino, he said. No more than five minutes away. A serviced apartment, not a house.'

'The Casino has serviced apartments. Why doesn't he lease one of them for the duration?'

'Too small. He wants something with enough room to entertain. And have guests to stay overnight.'

Lucille refrained from saying that he only needed one bed for that. Or was he into orgies?

'How many bedrooms?' she asked.

'Three at least, I'd say, to be on the safe side.'

'And what budget are we looking at?'

'Money is no object.'

Naturally not, Lucille thought caustically. Men like

Val Seymour thought they could buy anything they wanted.

And mostly they could.

'In that case, I don't see any problem. There's a beautifully appointed and serviced apartment ready for leasing in a new building just a short walk from the Casino. One of the reasons it hasn't been snapped up so far is that the owner has an exorbitantly high rental on it. But, if money is no object, Mr Seymour should be settled on the superb slate terrace, sipping a cocktail with his current lady-love, before the sun sets on Sydney Harbour.'

Erica chuckled. 'You *do* know Val.'

'His reputation does precede him,' Lucille said drily.

'Mmm. He *is* gorgeous, though. If I were only ten years younger…'

She'd probably be sleeping with *both* Seymour men, Lucille conceded. Her boss was a woman of the world, all right. But Lucille did admire her for the way she'd survived—and succeeded—after her divorce. The only thing that surprised Lucille was that Erica still liked men so much. Or was it just the sex she liked?

'I gather darling Val's actually ladyless at the moment,' Erica went on, rather confirming Lucille's suspicion that Flame had chosen the father over the son. 'So I'd watch him this afternoon, if were you. Max's son is not the sort of man to sleep alone for long, and you're a very good-looking woman, Lucille.'

A cold little laugh bubbled up from her throat. 'Thank you, but I don't think you have to worry about me falling for Val Seymour's rather over-used charms.'

'Don't be so sure. You haven't actually met him, have you?'

'No. But I've seen photos. I already know he's very handsome.'

'Not the same as seeing the real thing in the flesh, darling. Believe me. Now, how soon can you be here to pick up Don Juan for an inspection?'

'I thought he was going to take it, sight unseen.'

'Just a sec. I'll go into the lounge-room and ask...'

Lucille hung on for a good thirty seconds before Erica came back on the line.

'No, he says he always likes to see something first-hand, before he puts his money down.'

Lucille didn't doubt it. She wondered if he had potential girlfriends strip naked before he took them out. After all, the man was used to the very best. No point in wasting good money on dinner if the afters didn't rate a perfect ten.

'I'll have to get the keys from the agent first,' she said, and glanced at her watch. It was a quarter to two. 'Shall we say two-thirty?'

'Two-thirty okay, Val?' Lucille heard Erica ask.

'Can't she make it sooner than that?' came back the impatient reply. 'I thought you said your office was only up the bloody road.'

'It is. Can you get here any quicker, Lucille?'

'No, I can't,' she returned with superbly controlled cool. 'Tell Mr Seymour he'll just have to wait. Give him time to calm down and find some better language.'

Erica was laughing as she hung up, but frowning when she opened the front door to Lucille at a quarter to three.

'Not many women keep Val Seymour waiting this long, you know. He's about to burst a boiler.'

Lucille shrugged. 'It wasn't deliberate. The council's digging up the top of your road. Only one-way traffic. Sorry.'

'Never mind. I tried to improve his ill-humour by telling him that you were a ravishingly beautiful blonde, recently divorced, and not dating anyone that I knew of.'

Lucille was taken aback. 'Why on earth did you do that?'

'Why not? You're divorced, darling, not dead. Time to get back in the saddle, don't you think? And who better to ride than a man like Val Seymour?'

Lucille shuddered. She couldn't think of anything more revolting.

'You know, I was like you for simply ages after my divorce,' Erica persisted, 'but then I met darling Max and he showed me that men and sex could actually be fun. Something I'd long forgotten.'

Lucille could not believe she was having this conversation. She'd never exchanged intimate confidences with her boss and didn't want to now.

But neither did she want to offend her employer. Erica probably meant well.

'I'm sorry,' she said stiffly. 'But as it so happens, I simply can't stand the playboy type. They represent everything I detest in the male sex.'

'No, darling, you're wrong there. They represent everything you detest in a *husband*. But as a companion and lover, a playboy is simply the best. Men like Max and Val know how to give a girl a good time, both in bed and out. They know all the right moves, as well as all the right restaurants. They don't mind spending money on you, either. For divorcees like you and me they're ideal.'

'Thank you for the advice, Erica,' Lucille said, trying not to sound too annoyed, 'but I'm not interested in taking *any* lover just yet. It's much too soon.'

Erica's hard blue eyes softened a fraction. 'Fair enough. He must have been a right bastard, that husband of yours. Come on, then, let's go get the impatient Mr Seymour out of here. He's pacing again, and when Val paces, he practically wears grooves in the carpet.'

Lucille was only too happy to do just that, and terminate this irritating conversation. Bad enough that Michele was pushing her to date. Now her boss was suggesting she sleep with some over-sexed womaniser just for the *fun* of it!

Lucille couldn't see any fun in sleeping with a man she didn't respect. Even if she was interested in having a sex life, she wouldn't be seen dead as some playboy's pet! She'd choose a decent and more discreet lover, who wouldn't expect her to perform on cue simply because he spent swags of money on her.

Gritting her teeth, Lucille followed her boss inside, leaving the front door open behind her for a quick exit.

The lower floor of Erica's home was split-level and open plan: vast expanses of white-walled rooms, black-beamed ceilings and deep red carpet. Lucille trailed after Erica across the acre of foyer to where several curved steps led down into a huge sunken lounge-room.

When Erica stopped on the top step, Lucille drew alongside her.

'You do see what I mean, though, don't you?' Erica whispered, nodding towards the man in question, who was wearing a path in front of the picture window below, oblivious of the magnificent view of the harbour beyond.

Lucille saw *exactly* what Erica meant. A one-dimensional photograph couldn't possibly capture this man's person, or personality. His restless energy. His animal litheness and grace. His sheer sexual magnetism.

He was pacing up and down, up and down, his hands sunk deep in his trouser pockets, his stride as long as his legs. His dark head was lowered, his attitude one of prowling menace, his pantherish aura enhanced by his wearing black from head to toe. Black trousers. Black crew-necked top. Black shoes and socks.

He reminded Lucille of a big black cat she'd once seen in Taronga Park Zoo, pacing up and down his too small enclosure, exuding a threatening air of suppressed violence.

As a child, Lucille had found the animal quite frightening, despite the security fence between them.

Val Seymour looked as wild as that jungle cat. And there was no security fence around him.

Just as well I'm no longer a child, Lucille thought caustically.

Still he was a sexy-looking beast. She'd give him that. Once upon a time she might have found him incredibly attractive. Once upon a time she hadn't been immune to men.

'You're right,' she murmured ruefully to her boss.

'I'd better get him out of here before you have to replace the carpet.'

When Erica laughed, her visitor ground to a halt and glowered up at the pair of them.

Lucille flinched slightly at the impact of his piercing black eyes, framed as they were by his dark brows and a face which was as untamed-looking as the rest of him. He obviously hadn't shaved for a few days. Neither had he brushed his hair.

She wondered drily if the designer stubble and messily spiked hairstyle were deliberate. Who knew, these days? Whatever, he looked as if he'd just climbed out of bed after a long weekend of drink and debauchery.

'Lucille's sorry she's late,' Erica said as she hurried down into the lounge-room. 'Roadworks.'

Lucille followed her boss at a slower pace, wary of catching her stiletto heels in the thickly carpeted steps. No way was she going to risk a humiliating stumble in front of the likes of Val Seymour.

His brooding black gaze followed her every step, raking her from head to toe before lingering on her slender ankles and saucily shod feet. One of his dark brows arched slightly.

When his eyes lifted back to her face, she held them unswervingly, determined not to feel in any way undermined—or unnerved—by his physical appraisal of her.

'Lucille Jordan,' she said with cool politeness as she came forward and held out her hand.

Almost reluctantly, he fished his right hand out of his pocket and briefly shook hers. 'Val Seymour,' came his curt rejoinder. 'Can we get going straight away?'

'By all means.'

'Good. Thanks for the bolthole, Erica. And the help. I owe you one,' he tossed over his shoulder as he headed for the front door, leaping up the steps in a single bound.

'Oh, goodie,' Erica muttered salaciously under her breath, her eyes fixed on Val Seymour's very nice backside.

Lucille rolled her eyes and hurried after her rapidly departing client.

CHAPTER THREE

AFTER a slight detour to circumvent the roadworks, it was only a ten-minute drive across the bridge and over to their destination at Darling Harbour, especially at this time of day. Peak hour traffic hadn't yet begun to build.

But it seemed endless.

As much as she'd been determined not to be unnerved by Val Seymour's intimidating male presence, Lucille found herself becoming more and more tense with each passing second.

If only he would say something, instead of just sitting there in a darkly brooding silence with his head tipped back against the seat, his eyes shut and his arms grimly folded. Lucille couldn't make out if he was exhausted, or just being abominably rude.

Whatever, some light, ice-breaking conversation on her part wouldn't have gone astray. But be damned if she was going to be the first to speak.

So the seconds ticked slowly away and Lucille's irritation increased. By the time she steered her Oxford-green Falcon into one of the guest bays in the underground car park of their destination, she was seriously on edge.

'We're here,' she brusquely informed her seemingly sleeping passenger as she turned off the ignition. When he made no immediate move, or reply, she exhaled a deep and weary-sounding sigh.

His eyes half opened and slanted over to meet hers. 'That's exactly how I'm feeling at the moment,' he murmured. 'Tired to the bone. Are you tired too, Lucille? Or are you simply wishing Erica hadn't fostered such an impossible pain in the neck onto you for the afternoon?'

Everything he said flustered her inside, but especially his softly-voiced use of her Christian name. He had a lovely voice when he wasn't snapping and snarling. Low and warm and sensual. Her name had rolled off his tongue like liquid chocolate. His eyes were sensual too, when half opened in that heavy-lidded way.

He would look like that after he made love…

'No, not at all,' she denied with seeming calm whilst her thoughts went simply haywire. 'I get a little tense driving through the city centre, that's all,' she added by way of an excuse, struggling to regain her inner composure.

But the images of him lying next to her in bed persisted. Which was perverse. Val Seymour was the last man on earth she would want as her lover! Heavens, till this very moment, she hadn't wanted *any* man as her lover.

Lucille looked into his lazily hooded eyes and was suddenly seized by more than a spark. It was an inferno, spreading all through her body, melting her frozen libido and giving her a thirst for things she thought she'd never thirst for ever again.

It took an enormous effort of will to look away from him. 'Most people I deal with are under some kind of stress, Mr Seymour,' she elaborated as she removed her car key and retrieved her purse from the back seat.

By the time she glanced back into his face, her eyes were quite composed, though she couldn't say the same for the rest of her. 'It's my job to alleviate that stress by placing them in just the right accommodation. I'm sure you're going to be thrilled with this apartment. It has everything you're looking for. And more.'

He smiled a wry smile and sat up straight. 'Erica said you were her best consultant and I can see what she means. You have great tact and stay cool in the face of rudeness—which is what I've been up till now. Please accept my apology. I've had a difficult weekend followed by an even more difficult day. Which is no real excuse for my boorish behaviour, but it's all I have to offer. I'll try to be more congenial for the rest of the afternoon, but I can't promise perfection. And it's Val, all right? Mr Seymour sounds like my father, and, believe me, the last person on earth I want to be reminded of at this moment is him. Fair enough?'

'Fair enough,' she agreed, successfully hiding her ongoing inner turmoil with a plastic smile. Thank God he had no idea of the thoughts still tumbling through her head. Where on earth had they come from?

It was all Michele's and Erica's fault, Lucille decided angrily. They'd put them into her mind. All that talk of lovers and libido! And then there was the man himself. He was something else, as Erica had pointed out. Sex on two legs. A walking woman-trap. Those eyes! And that mouth!

'Right,' the object of her agitation said as he unsnapped his seat belt and threw open the car door. 'Let's go check out this apartment. Though if you claim it's perfect for me, Lucille, then no doubt it will be. A man would be a fool not to trust the judgement of a lady of your beauty and intelligence.'

He was out of the car in a flash, leaving her floundering after these last remarks. Common sense warned her that compliments to women would be an automatic part of his playboy arsenal, but why was he bothering to use them on *her*? She wasn't his usual style of bedmate.

Was he looking for an easy bolster for his bruised ego? An afternoon quickie to soothe the savage beast?

Such a prospect didn't repulse her nearly as much as it should have.

Oh, God.

She struggled out in her high heels, then cringed with embarrassment when she pointed the hand-held lock at the car and zapped the boot open instead of the doors closed.

'Botheration,' she muttered, hurrying forward to manually close the boot, then re-zap the doors.

'I do that all the time,' he said, materialising by her side with the stealth of a cat. 'When I drive, that is. Which isn't often. I don't own a car. I travel too much to be bothered. I usually borrow one of Max's when I'm in Sydney, but be damned if I will be this time. Sorry,' he said with a quick smile. 'Would you believe me if I said I don't usually swear in front of ladies?'

Lucille didn't. She'd already heard him swearing over the phone. Val Seymour was a man who did what he wanted, when he wanted, in front of whoever he wanted. He was being charming with a purpose in mind. She was sure of it. But *what* purpose? Seduction?

'I've heard worse,' she returned coolly, determined not to surrender to his easy charm.

His eyes glinted as they locked with hers. 'You have? I'm surprised anyone would dare in your presence.'

Her shoulders squared defensively. 'And what do you mean by that?'

'You have a formidable air about you, Lucille. Somewhere between ice princess and stern headmistress. Though the shoes are a bit of a worry. They don't fit either scenario.'

She blushed. She actually blushed.

He looked startled, and then confused. 'I'm sorry. That was rude of me. Again. Yet I'd just resolved to be polite.' His expression of bewilderment had a boyish quality about it which was even more dangerously attractive than his rampant sexuality. 'I'm not having a good day, am I?' he said with a sigh. 'Forgive me?'

'There's nothing to forgive,' came her starchy reply. 'The client is always right.'

'Ouch. Now I feel really guilty. Perhaps we should just get on with the inspection. Then I can say yes straight away, give you my credit card number and move straight in. After which you can be on your way and out of my reprehensible presence. Unless, of course, you need to check my references before I can take possession?'

His words took on a wicked double entendre in Lucille's erotically charged brain. But instead of being shocked, this time she felt nothing but a warped amusement. How ironic that this man of all men could turn her on! It was truly laughable.

'Mr Seymour,' she chided drily. 'You are being facetious.'

'Would I do that?' He smiled at her.

She couldn't help it. She simply couldn't keep up the ice princess act. Or was it the stern headmistress? She heartily disapproved of Val Seymour, and everything he stood for, but his charm was irresistible.

Her smile was still slow in coming, teasing the corners of her mouth before she finally surrendered to its pull.

His dark eyes danced at the sight of it, and her stomach flipped right over. The man was a devil, all right. An attractive and dangerous devil.

'Does that mean I'm forgiven?' he enquired flirtatiously.

Lucille decided enough was enough. She had to quickly regain control of this situation or she would be in deep trouble. As much as she might have been mentally fantasising about Val Seymour becoming her lover, she refused to let it actually happen. Pride demanded she keep him at bay and not do anything she might seriously regret.

'Mr Seymour—' she began in a businesslike tone.

'Val,' he corrected.

'Val…'

'Yes, Lucille?'

Why, oh, why did he choose that precise moment to say her name again? And to look at her like that again. With a warm, teasing smile and sparkling black eyes.

She shook her head in frustrated denial of his ongoing effect on her. 'You are a truly irritating man.'

'In what way?' he asked, his very real puzzlement as disarming as his natural charm.

'I was determined not to like you at all.'

Oh, God, had she really said that?

Now he was truly taken aback. 'I'm flattered. But was that a compliment or a criticism?'

'A fact,' she snapped, annoyed with herself.

'Well, I like you too,' he returned, looking amused. 'But I had no bad preconceptions of your character to battle against. You'll have to tell me over dinner tonight just what terrible things you'd heard about me that made you determined not to like me.'

Her mouth went instantly dry. 'Dinner tonight?'

'You have another engagement?'

'No, but...'

'Erica said you weren't dating anyone at the moment.'

'No, but...'

'Neither am I, if that's what's worrying you.'

'No, but...'

'No more buts, Lucille. You're coming to dinner with me tonight and that's that.'

Lucille could not contain a burst of exasperation. 'Did it ever occur to you that I may not *want* to come to dinner with you tonight?'

The expression on his face was classic. Lucille wondered if any woman had ever said no to him.

But then she remembered Flame.

Flame's defection was probably why *she* was being asked out in the first place. Loverboy needed his male ego stroking. Fast.

The thought piqued her own ego. 'I was going to put a treatment in my hair tonight,' she lied.

His eyes lifted to her hair, which had had the works at Janine's only the week before and was shining with health. 'It doesn't look like it needs one, but if you simply must, you could always do that before I pick you up. I never eat till late.'

Lucille almost rolled her eyes. *He* never ate till late. What was it with men that they never thought of anyone else's time-table but their own?

'I was planning on visiting my mother,' she persisted in prickly tones.

'You can do that another night.'

'What if she's ill in hospital?'

'*Is* she?'

'No, but what if she *was*?' she challenged.

'I'd buy her flowers and come with you. Then, afterwards, I'd take you to dinner.'

She sighed and gave up that tack. '*Why* do you want to take me to dinner? And I want the truth.'

He smiled that incredible smile of his. 'The truth, the whole truth and nothing but the truth?'

'Yes.'

'If you have to ask, then maybe you should have your sight checked. You're a beautiful woman, Lucille. I like beautiful women. And I like taking beautiful women to dinner.'

So there it was, in a nutshell. If she'd been plain, he wouldn't have asked her. The man's motives were skin-deep. What else?

Lucille knew that if she went to dinner with Val Seymour he would surely make a pass before the night was out. Given her sexual responses to him so far today, she didn't stand a chance in Hades of resisting him if he went into seduction mode. No point in kidding herself.

Lucille might have been out of the dating game for a good few years but she knew the score. Even ordinary thirty-something guys expected sex in exchange for the privilege of buying you some wine and a meal these days. A playboy like Val Seymour would consider it a foregone conclusion. Saying yes to dinner would be the same as agreeing to a one-night stand with him.

Given Lucille's present vulnerability to the man, it was an incredibly corrupting thought.

'Can I take a few minutes to think about it?' she said, trying to sound cool and not panic-stricken.

Again, he looked surprised. But he recovered quickly, to flash her a warm smile. 'Yeah. Sure. Take all the time you want. Meanwhile, let's go look at my new digs.'

He took her arm on the walk across the car park to the lift, the touch of his hand doing incredible things to her whole body. Goosebumps erupted all over her skin and her heartbeat took off at a wild gallop.

Lord help me, she thought.

His hand dropped away in the lift, for which she was grateful, as she was for the talkative couple who got on at lobby level. The apartment they were to inspect was on the twelfth floor, by which time the lift was again empty, except for themselves.

'I presume this place has a good view of Sydney,' Val remarked when the lift stopped and they alighted onto a grey-carpeted corridor.

'One hundred and eighty degrees,' she answered matter-of-factly. 'The Casino on the left, the Darling

Harbour complex and Marina directly opposite, and
the central business district on the right.'

'It *does* sound perfect,' he agreed.

And perfect it was, provided you liked blue. That
colour dominated every room, ranging from the palest
ice-blue to a bold navy. The walls, the floor coverings,
the bench-tops, the soft furnishings. They were all blue
in one shade or other. Sometimes the brighter, darker
blues were combined and softened with grey. In other
places the designer had contrasted them with white.
White woodwork. White appliances in the kitchen.
White lampshades and cushions.

The rooms were spacious, the furniture sleek and
expensive, yet comfy and liveable. Huge squashy
leather sofas and chairs. Roomy tables. Big beds.

There was a *very* big bed in the main bedroom. A
very big spa bath as well. Large enough for the most
decadent of orgies.

'Now, that's my kind of bath,' Val remarked on
seeing it, and Lucille tried not to think of his climbing
into the darned thing with a bevy of naked beauties.

The bath, however, was not as big a hit as the terrace, which stretched the entire length of the best side
of the building and was wide enough to easily accom-
modate the plethora of white wrought-iron furniture,
grouped in several settings over the grey slate floor.
Large white-painted pots filled with amazingly real-
looking ferns gave it a summery resort-style look, and
a built-in slate barbecue made it perfect for entertain-
ing on balmy summer evenings.

Not this evening, however. A brisk breeze was
blowing up from the water, promising a cool spring
night and messing up Lucille's hair.

Val's hair, however, remained impervious to the wind. It stayed exactly as it was, totally messy and looking sexy as hell.

'You're right, Lucille,' he said as he leant against the curved grey railing and soaked up the panoramic view. 'I could happily live in this place. What's the damage?' he asked, glancing her way.

'The damage?' she echoed, having tuned out momentarily. She'd been too busy watching him move, and thinking the wickedest of thoughts.

'How much does it cost?'

'I thought money was no object,' she reminded him stiffly, positioning herself so that her hair blew back from her face and not across it.

'It isn't. I just want to know how much this is going to cost Max. I'll be charging it to the company's expense account.'

'Four thousand a week,' she said, and he grimaced.

'Not nearly enough.'

'That's the flat rate. It'll climb once you add on the other services provided.'

When his eyebrows arched, she slanted him a droll look. 'Sorry. Not that kind of service. I was talking about cleaning and meals and Internet shopping and such.'

'You mean I won't have to lift a finger?'

'Only to open the champagne, which of course can also be ordered from here. Actually, you don't even have to open the bottles if you don't want to. There's a butler service as well.'

His rather patrician nose wrinkled at this idea. 'I'm not really into that sort of thing. But the champagne is a good idea. I'll order a case. Dom Perignon, of course,' he added with a wicked grin.

'Your father really isn't in your good books at the moment, is he?'

'My father doesn't know the meaning of good,' he scoffed, then glowered, his mood dropping back into black and brooding. 'I don't want to talk about that bastard. I don't even want to *think* about him.' He sank back down against the railing, his head sagging, his attitude one of instant and utter wretchedness.

For a brief moment Lucille actually felt sorry for him, till she remembered that he was a bastard too, especially with women.

So this time he'd lost out with Flame, a potential bedmate. Tough! It wasn't as though he'd been genuinely in love with the girl. Playboys like Val Seymour were only in love with themselves!

He straightened abruptly and turned to face her, his eyes still tormented.

Amazing how devastatingly attractive he looked, despite his emotional ravagement. The dark circles under his eyes suited his designer stubble and added to his bad-boy image.

'Are you going to put me out of my misery by coming to dinner with me tonight, Lucille?' he demanded to know. 'Or are you going to condemn me to eternal depression?'

'How will a date with me put you out of your misery?' she challenged, as if she didn't know. A conquest a day keeps depression at bay!

'It just will,' he said firmly. 'I promise to be a gentleman, if that's what's worrying you. Just dinner and conversation. Nothing else.'

Lucille frowned. He actually *sounded* sincere. Who knew? Maybe he meant the 'just dinner' part. Maybe he simply wanted the distraction of company. Maybe he *had* been in love with that Flame female and was genuinely upset.

Lucille was startled to find she didn't like that last thought. Perhaps because underneath she wanted him to want her as she wanted him. Oh, yes, there was no point in denying it, not to herself. She wanted him. Wanted him naked, wanted him in bed, wanted him right now, or at the very latest…tonight.

Any shock—or self-disgust—at this starkly explicit realisation was eventually overlaid by an angrily defensive train of thought. Why shouldn't she want him? And why shouldn't she have him, at least once? Now that her female hormones were up and running again, she'd be stupid not to take advantage of this situation. Erica was right. Who better to have sex with than a man who specialised in the practice?

It wasn't as though Val would be hurt by her going to bed with him. Hell, he'd probably be grateful.

A decidedly erotic quiver ran down her spine at the thought. Despite his promise of gentlemanly behaviour, Lucille knew that a virile man like Val didn't stand a chance of staying virtuous if she pulled out all the stops, then didn't say no when he took the bait.

'All right,' she said, amazed that she could sound so calm in the face of such wicked plottings. 'I wouldn't want to be responsible for plunging you into eternal depression.'

'Fantastic,' he said, finding an instant smile.

Lucille smiled back. I've gone mad, she decided. Stark raving mad.

Whatever was Michele going to say?

Nothing, the devil's voice whispered in Lucille's head. Because you're not going to tell her. Tonight is going to be your dark little secret. Your deep, dark little secret.

CHAPTER FOUR

HER phone rang at ten to eight, just as she was doing some last-minute frantic primping.

'What a time for someone to ring,' Lucille muttered as she hurried from her bedroom to the living-room.

Not that she hadn't already had three hours to get ready since arriving home at five. But three hours simply weren't enough for this kind of date. There was so much to be done. So much to be worried over, and to change her mind over. Not the least of which was what one should wear to seduce a man who'd been seduced by the best of them.

In the end she'd gone for broke, in a dress which would have revived an octogenarian on life support. It was part of the wardrobe she'd splurged on after her divorce had come through but never worn. Emerald chiffon with a low-cut V neckline, sheer tight sleeves and a softly layered skirt which fell to mid-calf, leaving her slender ankles and sexily shod feet in full view. Her cleavage was deep and her hair up in a fashionably dishevelled style, with tendrils falling all round her neck.

Lucille swept the receiver up to her ear, clinking with one of the crystal drop earrings she'd just hooked into her lobes.

'Yes?' she said sharply down the line.

'It's Val. I'm stuck in a traffic snarl on the bridge. I'm going to be late getting to your place.'

Hearing his voice brought home exactly what she was doing. This wasn't some wild sexual fantasy she was about to embark on. This was a real man she was planning to seduce. And she was a real woman. A woman who hadn't made love in so long she'd probably forgotten how!

Lucille's stomach crunched down hard, then churned. She couldn't go through with this. She simply couldn't. What had she been thinking of? Aside from any other consideration, the man was a playboy, for pity's sake. Maybe he *would* know all the right moves in bed, as Erica had pointed out. But her pride simply wouldn't allow herself to let such a man think she was nothing but an easy lay.

Which he would.

'Lucille?' he prompted.

'Yes, I'm here,' she said stiffly. At least she would have time to change again, into something less provocative.

'Sorry about this,' he said.

'It can't be helped. You needn't have worried. Or called.'

'I didn't want you to think I was deliberately keeping you waiting, or that I was an arrogant creep with no respect for time or women.'

'I wouldn't have thought that,' she bit out, though she probably would have.

'You sound a little upset.'

'Not at all. I'm just not ready yet.'

His laugh was low and incredibly sexy, reminding Lucille of why she'd been brought to this.

'Now I understand,' he said. 'I sometimes forget it takes women for ever to get dressed. Off you go, then, because I want you ready and waiting when I arrive. I'm literally starving.'

She bristled. 'I thought you said you always ate late.'

'I seem to have forgotten to eat today, and the cupboards in my new apartment were bare, except for coffee and tea.'

'Oh, dear. I should have seen to that.'

'That's what Erica said when I called to thank her for everything. But don't fret. I soothed her concerns by saying I was going out for dinner tonight and you'd promised to attend to the matter first thing in the morning.'

Lucille's heart missed a beat. 'You didn't tell her you were taking *me* out to dinner, did you?'

'No...'

'Thank God.'

'Why?'

'Why what?'

'Why didn't you want me to tell her?'

Lucille didn't know what to say.

'I have an awful feeling,' Val went on drily, after an embarrassing stretch of silence, 'that your reluctance to answer has something to do with your poor opinion of my character.'

Lucille didn't deny it.

'Mmm. We will explore this subject more in depth over dinner, when you can't get away with going silent on me. Ah, the traffic's moving. I might not be too long after all. Better shake a leg, Lucille, or you'll be going to dinner in whatever you have on at the moment. Dare I hope it's your birthday suit?'

She *did* end up going to dinner in what she had on

at that moment, because Erica rang as soon as she hung up, chastising her for not catering to Val's basic culinary needs on the spot, after which she tried to pump Lucille for her personal opinion of the man. By the time Lucille had neatly side-stepped her boss's questions and got off the darned phone, it was too late to change. Her intercom buzzer began ringing before she could take more than two steps back towards her bedroom.

Lucille groaned, accepting ruefully that she would have to go to dinner as she was. Hopefully Val wouldn't get the wrong idea about the way she looked. Not that she was all *that* provocatively dressed by modern standards. Val was probably used to his dates wearing a whole lot less. As long as she didn't *act* provocatively, or flirtatiously, he would have no reason to get out of line.

The dangly earrings could go, however, she decided sensibly, unhooking and tossing them on the hall table as she hurried past on her way to the intercom beside the front door. Now that she'd come to her senses she could hardly believe that her self-esteem had let her sink so low as to actually consider throwing herself at such a man.

If she'd been able to politely get out of dinner, she would have. A bit hard, however, when he was right downstairs and she'd only spoken to him minutes before. All she could do was keep her defences in place and not let him get to her sexually a second time.

'That you, Val?' she said coolly, on flipping the switch.

'The one and only. All dressed and raring to go?'

'Just about.' All she had to do was get her purse. 'I

won't be more than a minute. You might as well wait down there.'

'Fine.'

Lucille contemplated changing her shoes, but that old rebellious streak won out and she didn't. A mistake, possibly, she worried as she rode the lift down to the lobby. The black patent high heels gracing her feet tonight made today's cream stilletos look sedate. Not because they were higher. That would have been impossible. But because of the amount of exposed foot. There was only one pencil-thin strap anchoring her foot to the sole and another wickedly sinful one snaking around her ankle. They were painful shoes to wear, but made her feet look gorgeous and her sleekly stockinged legs even better.

Val certainly seemed to think so when he caught sight of her stepping out of the lift. He was standing outside, under the covered porch, but had a perfect view through the glass security doors of the building's lobby area. His eyes followed her every step as she walked towards him, his gaze riveted to her lower legs.

Lucille was staring at him too, but he was too intent on her ankles and shoes to notice.

He'd changed clothes since she'd left him, though he was still wearing black. Black tailored trousers. Black silk shirt which buttoned right up to his neck. Black belt and shoes.

Clearly his father's housekeeper had hopped to it and done Val's bidding. Just before Lucille had left him this afternoon Val had rung the woman and asked her to send all his things over in a taxi.

Lucille suspected that most women did Val's bidding. Pronto.

He'd also showered and shaved since she'd last seen him. Brushed his hair too. Where before he'd been roughly handsome, now he was smoothly handsome. Dazzlingly so.

Lucille might have been dazzled if she hadn't been ready for her sexual reaction this time. Her heartbeat still quickened but her defences remained in place, swiftly dispensing with the sudden silly idea that Val's interest in her might not be transitory or superficial.

Playboys don't date little nobodies like you, she reminded herself. Their girlfriends are supermodels. Heiresses. Pop stars. Actresses. This was obviously a spur-of-the-moment invitation. Val needed the distraction of company tonight and you just happened to be there.

A cynical conclusion, but then Lucille *was* cynical about men. She had every reason to be.

Still, he seemed to genuinely like what he was seeing tonight. More than like. His eyes were gleaming with male admiration as she swung open one of the glass doors. Lucille's female self couldn't help feeling flattered by his fancying her physically, but she wasn't about to get carried away. She'd dressed to attract him, after all.

'Wow,' he said, finally glancing back up into her face. 'Now the rest of you matches the shoes.'

Lucille smiled a sardonic smile. He had no idea how much she'd matched those shoes a few short minutes before. If she'd remained in her earlier erotically inflamed mood, seeing him looking this gorgeous himself would probably have heated her up so far she would have been in danger of spontaneous combustion.

As it was, she could still detect some body changes she seemed to have no control over. A tingling all over the surface of her skin. A tightness in places which hadn't been tight a few seconds before. That insidious quickening of her heartbeat.

Just as well nothing was visible to the naked eye.

'What happened to the ice princess?' he asked, smiling.

'I always put the ice princess to bed after the sun goes down,' she tossed back blithely.

'And the stern headmistress?' he enquired.

She met his dancing black eyes with cool green ones. 'She's there, ready and waiting, if my date gets out of line.'

He grinned, then gave her considerable cleavage an appreciative once-over. 'If you wear dresses like that on your dates, I'll bet a good few get out of line.'

She ignored *that* one. 'Actually, I haven't dated for a while.'

'Ah, yes, Erica said as much earlier this afternoon. Why not?'

Her shrug was splendidly nonchalant. 'No spark.'

He frowned. 'No spark?'

'That's right.'

His eyebrows arched. 'Does that mean there's a spark with me?'

Her smile was dry. 'Come now, Val, a girl would have to be myopic or a moron not to feel at least a tiny spark with a man of your many God-given talents.'

His brows dropped, then beetled together. 'Why do I get the feeling that's a criticism again, and not a compliment?'

'I have no idea. Maybe you're paranoid.'

He shook his head, clearly frustrated by her cryptic repartee. 'Not usually, but I suspect I could get that way around you.'

'Oh, dear,' she murmured as he steered her over to the waiting taxi. 'We can't have that.'

She felt his puzzled frown on her as she climbed in, and she *did* feel a bit guilty. Open sarcasm wasn't usually her way.

But underneath she did so resent his effortless charm, and the way he made her feel. Damn it all, why couldn't her libido have been unfrozen by an or-dinary guy? Why did it have to be a womanising play-boy? She wouldn't have had to resist a regular guy. She could have surrendered to what she wanted with-out having to feel disgustingly weak, or appallingly cheap, or just plain foolish.

She could only hope that when this night was over she wouldn't revert to the woman she'd been before meeting Val Seymour. Because Michele was so right. She didn't really want to be alone and celibate for the rest of her life. It was too lonely. Too…unnatural.

Or so it seemed at the moment, with Val pressed so close to her in the back of the taxi. His maleness seemed to be calling out to her, making her brutally aware of her woman's body, especially those parts she'd fantasised about him touching, and kissing, and caressing. Her breasts. Her belly. Her bottom.

Her eyes slid sidewards to lock with his, his smoul-dering gaze sending every hormonally activated nerve-ending in her body off the Richter scale of arousal. When he began to lean her way she was sure he was going to kiss her, and, whilst the prospect produced an instant panic, she knew she wouldn't stop him.

He must have picked up on her alarmed body language, however, because he didn't kiss her. Instead, he smiled a wry smile and shifted away a little.

'Sorry,' he drawled. 'Didn't mean to invade your personal space. I'll keep a more gentlemanly distance in future.'

Lucille didn't know if she felt relief or dismay.

In the end, self-irritation overrode everything else. To think she would have let him kiss her! Just like that! Lord, she'd have to be careful in the taxi after dinner. And when he walked her to the door. There'd be no coming up for coffee. Or anything like that.

Being alone with this sexy devil could spell disaster, especially with some wine in both their systems. As much as she might have fantasised about it, no way was Lucille going to wake up the next morning with Val Seymour's head on the pillow beside her. No way!

Grimly determined to keep her own head from now on, she ordered her treacherous body to behave itself for the rest of the evening, then settled back to stare blankly through the passenger window at the city lights. Anything was better than looking at the man seated next to her. If she didn't want to make a complete fool of herself before this evening was out, then looking at him was best kept to a minimum!

But how on earth was she expected not to look at him in the restaurant, when he'd be sitting right opposite her? There was only so much staring at menus that she could indulge in.

Lucille sighed. Saying yes to this dinner date had been a big, big mistake!

CHAPTER FIVE

THE restaurant was only five minutes away, an intimate little harbourside place with a view.

Lucille had asked Val to choose somewhere dimly lit and discreet, not one of those overpriced showy places where the famous and infamous went to see and be seen. Lucille cringed at the thought of appearing in any of the gossip columns as Val Seymour's latest ladylove.

She could see it now. *Dashing entrepreneur seen dining alone with mystery blonde.*

Despite all Val's precautions—he swore he'd never been here before—it was obvious the *maître d'* recognised him. They were unctuously shown to the best table in the house, over in a private and rather precious corner, with a screen protecting them from the other patrons but nothing between them and the truly spectacular night view of the harbour bridge and the city lights beyond.

On the plus side, no one gawked or whispered as they were shown to their privileged spot. In truth, the diners probably couldn't see all that well beyond the immediate circle of their own tables, the room was so subtly lit—the result of tiny recessed ceiling lights and only a single candle sitting on each dark-clothed table.

Lucille smiled ruefully to herself as she sat down, remembering what Michele had said about candlelit dinners putting a girl in the mood. Little did Michele

52

know, but a man like Val didn't need romantic accompaniments to put a girl in the mood. All he had to do was turn up!

'What's tickling your fancy?' Val asked, looking up from the wine list he'd been handed.

'Just something a girlfriend said to me at lunch today,' she replied, thinking how devilishly attractive he looked by candlelight. If Satan himself had chosen to take flesh, then this was how he would look. Black hair. Black eyes. And a sinfully sexy mouth.

That sinfully sexy mouth smiled a sinfully sexy smile. 'Am I allowed to ask what?'

'Secret women's business is never shared with menfolk,' she replied haughtily.

'Oh, I see.' He nodded sagely. 'You were talking about sex.'

'Would an ice princess do that?' she mocked.

'I would think ice princesses talk about little else,' he countered. 'Because that's all they ever do on the subject. Talk.'

'You could be right there,' she confessed on a dry note.

He laughed. 'Somehow I don't think I'm even close. So what have we here?' he mused, running his eyes over the list of wines. 'Red or white?'

'Either. I like them both.'

'You trust me to choose the wine for you?' He sounded surprised.

'But of course. I'm sure wine-choosing is something you're very good at. Amongst lots of other things...'

He closed the folder with just a hint of exasperation. 'Are you having a shot at me again?'

Lucille shrugged. 'I was merely telling the truth.'

'Which is?'

'That a man of your...shall we say...*experience*?...would be very talented in all things sophisticated.'

'You sound like you don't approve of my...*experience*.'

'Not at all. I think experience in a man is very attractive.'

'In that case, it's me personally you don't approve of,' he concluded thoughtfully.

Lucille could not bring herself to deny what was a very true statement.

He frowned at her silence. 'I would have thought a woman as intelligent as yourself would not swallow all that garbage journalists write about me,' he ground out.

Lucille almost laughed. Surely he wasn't going to try that old chestnut, was he? 'Are you saying you and all the women you've been romantically linked with were just good friends?' she challenged.

'No. But my dear father often put around false rumours of affairs between me and the stars of our shows because he thought it was good for business. Perversely, it was. People gobble up that kind of gossip.'

'I find it hard to believe that *all* those stories about your stormy love-life with leading ladies were put-up jobs.'

'No, of course they weren't. I've had relationships with several leading ladies over the years. Some of them quite stormy.'

'And none of which lasted for very long,' she pointed out drily.

He shrugged. 'I'm a man, not a saint. And not always a gentleman, either,' he added drily. 'So, yes, I've been to bed with a few of the ladies in question. But believe me, they always knew the score. There were certainly no broken hearts left behind afterwards.'

'You were never in love with any of them?'

'I was possibly a little in love with all of them. They were passionate creatures, and passion is something which always gets me in. But, no, being truly in love is something I haven't had the privilege of experiencing as yet.'

Lucille suspected he wasn't losing any sleep over the fact.

'What about your father?' she asked tartly.

'What *about* my father?'

'Were a lot of the stories of *his* affairs over the years just clever advertising for his shows?'

'I do not wish to discuss my father's affairs,' he grated out. 'Not that I think of him as my father any more. Once my commitment to the present show is over and done with, I will have no more to do with him. I'm finished with Seymour Productions, and Max Seymour!'

Lucille was startled by the barely held fury in his voice. No wonder he empathised with passion. He was an incredibly passionate man. Suddenly, she could see his Latin American half in his body language. His hands moved expressively as he spoke, the red leather wine folder waved about whilst his black eyes flashed and blazed.

He got a grip with difficulty, but Lucille feared dinner was in danger of being spoiled. She was spoiling it with her cynical probing. And she really didn't want to do that. Despite everything, she was rather enjoying herself in a kind of perverse fashion.

'I'm sorry,' she said swiftly. 'I shouldn't have asked. It's none of my business, just as your love-life is none of my business. As you said, this is just a dinner date.'

He glowered at her across the table before shaking his head and exhaling a frustrated sigh. 'At least I now know why you were hesitant in coming out with me. You think I'm a heartless womaniser, just like my father.'

Lucille did, but decided it was wise to hold her tongue at this juncture.

'I am *nothing* like my father,' he ground out. 'That man should have his heart cut out. He has no conscience. All he knows is his own selfish wants and desires. He doesn't care who he hurts, just so long as his own enormous ego is gratified. I had no idea the man was such a monster till this last weekend.'

Lucille could not contain her curiosity. 'What did he do?' she asked with deceptive quietness. Inside, she was simply dying to know.

His black eyes blazed. 'What did he do? He betrayed a trust, that's what he did.'

'How?'

'To put it bluntly, he seduced a young woman I'd introduced to him, without caring how much it might hurt me, his son, the son he *claims* to love.'

So there it was. A virtual admission of what had transpired that weekend. Father and son wanting the same woman, with the father the victor and the son left with a bruised and battered ego.

For what else could it be? The concept that Val might be deeply in love with Flame didn't fit either his reputation or his own admission that he'd never been in love.

Still, she couldn't help feeling sorry for him. He did look distressed. And hurt. And disillusioned. To lose a girlfriend was one thing. To lose her to his father had to be hard to take.

Although not impressed with either father or son's lifestyles, Lucille could appreciate how it felt to have a parent let you down. She'd felt let down by hers. They'd never taken her side during her divorce. They'd never asked about or tried to understand what Roger had done to her. They'd just judged and criticised.

'You're talking about Flame, aren't you?' she said with compassion in her voice. And, yes, in her heart.

His eyes snapped up to hers. 'What in hell do *you* know about Flame? Has Erica been gossiping to you?'

'No! No, I just guessed. I saw the picture of her with you and your father in Sunday's paper. There was a large article about the dance show you're producing, plus its star.'

His scowl carried frustration. 'I'd forgotten they were printing that stupid story this weekend. Another of Max's brilliant ideas to advertise the show. I dare say the papers used that disgusting picture which made it look like we were having some kind of kinky *ménage à trois*. Well, we weren't! But, yes—yes, I'm talking about Flame. Though that's not her real name. It's Angela.'

'I presume this Angela was *your* girlfriend till this last weekend, then?'

'What? No. No, nothing like that,' he dismissed irritably. 'Hell, no. Is that what you've been thinking? Damn and blast. My father has more to answer for than I realised.'

He scowled and shook his head, his expression was one of black frustration. 'How to explain this without breaking confidences?' he muttered. 'Look, my relationship with Angela goes back a long way. You know I'm illegitimate, I presume?'

When she nodded, he laughed drily. 'Who doesn't? Max never hid the fact. I dare say you also know my mother was Brazilian. A nightclub dancer. Very beautiful. Very…flashy. Specialised in the tango. Anyway, my father had a brief affair with her one summer in Paris. He didn't know of my existence for twelve years. When my mother found out she was dying of cancer she contacted him and asked him if he'd take me. I don't think she thought he would, but she was desperate. By then she was very poor, you see. No longer dancing. No longer all that beautiful. No longer capable of working at all. She was back living in Rio and we were so darned poor. There wasn't the welfare payment there that people have in this country, you see.'

Lucille didn't want to hear the details of Val's early life. She didn't want to feel compassion for him. She didn't want to start understanding him, or liking him too much. She was already having difficulty resisting him.

'Where does Angela come into all this?' she asked a bit curtly, hoping to stop the flow of feelings he was evoking with his wretched story.

His eyes bored into her for a few seconds, then he

shrugged. 'Angela's mother and mine lived in the same house. We were like brother and sister. I used to mind her sometimes, when she was just a tiny tot. I became quite fond of her. When my father shocked everyone by actually turning up and taking me back to Australia to live with him, I kept in contact by letter but didn't see her again till recently. I'd heard about Brazil's latest dance sensation and decided to see if I could talk her into coming to Australia. You have no idea how shocked I was when Flame turned out to be Angela.'

'How old is she now?' Lucille asked.

'Twenty-five.'

'Hardly a child, Val.'

'Maybe not. But she's many years younger than my father. I thought she would be safe in my own home, but I was wrong. Hell, was I ever! I'd like to kill the bastard. Once this show is done I'm going abroad; I don't ever want to see him again.'

'Why don't you cut all ties now, if you hate him so much?'

'I wish I could, but I've given my word to produce this dance spectacular and I don't want to let people down.'

'People, Val? Or Angela?'

'There are many people involved, but, yes, I'm more concerned with Angela's future than the others. If I keep in personal contact with her, maybe I can coerce her out of my father's clutches.'

And into yours?

Lucille believed Val when he said Angela hadn't been his girlfriend first. But she suspected he'd wanted her to be. You only had to see the girl's photo to know that any man would be smitten by her darkly sensual beauty. It was obvious Val hadn't given up the idea of still having her for himself. Maybe that was another reason why he wanted to rent such an impressive—and very convenient—apartment. To have somewhere nearby to take this Angela between rehearsals, somewhere snazzy and seductive.

'I see,' she said.

Val's eyes narrowed at the cynical tone of those two little words.

'No. No, you *don't* see, Lucille. But *I* do. Well and truly.' His face took on a closed look, his eyes freezing to an icy black. 'Under the circumstances, there's absolutely no point in continuing this particular conversation, or in my trying to change your perception of me, or my character. I have one strict policy in life. Never to go—or stay—where I'm not wanted. Which is why I left my father's house. And why I am going to order the wine and get on with this dinner.'

CHAPTER SIX

THE evening was spoilt after that. Totally spoilt. Lucille went through the motions of drinking the wine Val ordered. And the meal *she* ordered.

But she might as well have been eating cardboard.

The conversation—what there was of it—was very general, and somewhat stilted. They touched briefly on the economy, real estate, the recent referendum. Even that old polite standby…the weather.

'Been raining a lot lately, hasn't it?'

'Do you think it's global warming?'

'Not much one can do about it, is there?'

'Buy shares in an umbrella company, I guess.'

By the time dessert was served Lucille wished she was anywhere else but there. A crypt would have been warmer than the atmosphere around their table. Val no longer looked at her with male admiration but with utter boredom. He'd emotionally and mentally removed himself to a distance from which he showed not the slightest real interest in anything she had to say.

'Do you want tea or coffee?' he asked idly when the waiter hovered once more.

Lucille couldn't bear the thought of prolonging this torture.

'No, thanks. I don't drink caffeine this close to going to bed.'

'Anything else, perhaps?' came the polite but off-hand query. 'A liqueur? Cognac?'

'No, thank you.'

'Fine,' he said crisply. 'The bill, please?' he asked the waiter.

Five minutes later they were in a taxi, speeding towards North Sydney.

'Don't worry about coming over to the apartment in the morning,' he said coldly when they were nearing her street. 'As you said, I can place a grocery order on the Internet.'

Lucille felt even more wretched, if that were possible. 'What will I tell Erica if she asks?'

'Tell her *you* did it. Tell her whatever you like.'

Suddenly, Lucille couldn't bear his coldness. Or was it his indifference she couldn't bear? 'Please don't be angry with me, Val.'

He sighed. 'I'm not. Not really. I'm more angry with myself. I never realised before tonight the price I would have to eventually pay for selecting the wrong man as my idol as an adolescent.'

'What do you mean?' Surely he wasn't truly *in love* with Angela.

'Nothing,' he muttered. 'I mean nothing. We're here. Do you want me to walk you to your door?'

'Only if you want to.'

'I'd like to come further than your damned door,' he muttered, then threw her a bitter smile. 'But, as I said before, I don't go where I'm not wanted.'

She stared at him. She could send him away, or take what he was subtly offering. It was entirely up to her.

Her mind struggled to find a balance between her pride and her physical desire for this man. If she had sex with Val she knew she would regret it in the morning. But if she didn't she had an awful feeling she might regret it for the rest of her life.

Maybe she'd never feel like this ever again. Maybe Val was what she needed to put the ice princess to bed once and for all. Erica had said as much, and she should know. She'd been in the same boat.

All Lucille had to remember was that it *was* just sex. Nothing more.

'Would you like to come upstairs for a cup of coffee?' she asked, pleased that her voice sounded pretty normal.

He stared at her, astonishment blending with wariness.

'I thought you said you didn't drink coffee before you went to bed.'

'That's only when I'm planning on sleeping.'

He stared at her even harder, then shook his head. 'Damn, but you're one complex lady.'

'Aren't we all?'

'Some are more complex than others.'

'Are you coming up or not?'

'Hell, honey, you don't have to ask me twice.' He paid the driver with a twenty-dollar note, then bundled her out of the taxi with almost indecent haste.

He really didn't give her much time for second thoughts as he steered her up the front steps of the building and over to the glass doors. But if her mind was momentarily bamboozled, her body wasn't. It was already up and running, her blood roaring around her veins, heat zooming into every erogenous zone she owned.

'Got your key handy?' he whispered, his lips brushing her earlobe.

Somehow, she found her key in her purse. He took it and did the honours, for which she was grateful, because she was fast becoming incapable of anything which required skills such as digital co-ordination. She could walk. Just. But inserting keys in locks was far too difficult a task for her desire-addled brain. All she could think of was Val, and how soon he would be kissing her, touching her, undressing her.

A violent shudder racked her whole body.

'Cold, sweetheart? Not to worry. I'll have you all warmed up in no time.'

She stifled a groan. How confident he was. How sexually assured. Whereas she...

What kind of lover was *she*?

A good one, she thought, once upon a time.

Certainly neither of her two boyfriends before Roger had ever complained. But then...they'd been mere boys. Still, Roger hadn't complained either, to begin with. In fact he'd seemed fascinated by her tendency to get really carried away when she was turned on. He hadn't been able to get enough of her in the beginning.

Yes, Roger had seemed more than happy with her passionate nature—till after they were married. Then everything had begun to change, both in bed and out...

'What floor?'

Lucille blinked back to reality to find them standing side by side in the lift, with Val's hand hovering over the potential buttons and his eyes steadfastly on hers.

'Oh. Er...first.'

He pressed the right button and the lift doors whirred closed.

'What on earth were you thinking about just then?' he asked.

'Nothing important.'

'Nothing nice, I suspect,' came his dry comment.

'I was thinking of my ex-husband.'

'Then don't think about him. Don't think about anything. Just kiss me.'

'*Kiss* you? *Here?*'

When the lift stopped Val held down the button to stop the doors from opening. 'I'm not leaving this lift till you kiss me,' he said with a dead serious face.

Lucille tried to stay calm, despite a madly galloping heart. 'You have a thing for kissing in lifts?'

'I have a thing for *you*. And it can't wait another moment.'

She stiffened. 'If you expect me to do it in a lift, then you can think again.'

'Don't go all ice princess on me again, honey. I prefer the secret woman I keep glimpsing, the one whose smouldering green eyes tell me a vastly different story.'

'Smouldering?' Lucille was taken aback by the word. She'd honestly thought she'd hidden her desire for him.

'You have no idea. Sometimes, those gorgeous green eyes of yours are so hot they burn right into me.'

Embarrassment curled Lucille's stomach and flushed her cheeks. 'I...I didn't realise.'

'I know. That's what makes you so intriguing.'

She shook her head. 'There's nothing intriguing about me.'

'You're wrong there. You're very intriguing. But I'm not about to play twenty questions with you just now. All I want for now is for you to kiss me.'

She wanted to too. She really did. But she just couldn't bring herself to take such an initiative. It had been too long and she felt too…insecure.

'I…I can't,' she choked out. 'I just can't.' She crossed her arms and hugged herself defensively. 'The truth is, Val, I…I haven't done anything like this before. And I'm just plain scared.'

'You've never done *what* before?' he asked, frowning.

'Had a one-night stand. Or an affair. Or any kind of sex at all. Not since I left my husband.'

'And when was that?'

'Almost two years ago now.'

'Good God.'

'I know. It's unnatural.'

'Unusual, perhaps, but there's nothing unnatural about you, Lucille. You're all woman. Still, under the circumstances, you certainly don't want a quickie in a lift. I think we should adjourn to the privacy of your place, don't you?'

It was a rhetorical question because he immediately let go the button, took her elbow and ushered her out through the rapidly opening doors. 'Which door is yours?'

'Number three,' she croaked, now truly petrified. 'Over there.'

He still had her keys, and had her inside before she could say Jack Robinson. Inside and being drawn into his arms, then being kissed as no man had *ever* kissed her before.

Lucille had imagined Val would be a passionate lover, with his Latin genes. But being on the end of such passion was way beyond her imagination.

He didn't kiss with just his lips and tongue. It was a full body experience. His hands were simply everywhere, caressing and pressing, moulding her soft curves around his steely self, forcing her to feel every inch of his instantly formidable erection.

For a few blinding, blistering seconds she just wallowed in his ardour, moaning under his deeply darting tongue and revelling in the feeling of being so wanted. But then that smouldering fire of hers he'd talked about ignited in full, and being a submissive partner was simply not enough.

Her purse slipped from her fingers to clatter at their feet and she lifted her arms to wind them around his neck, pressing herself closer to him, if that was possible. He groaned and spun her round, pushing her back against the wall. One of her legs lifted instinctively to rub along his outer thigh, her hips undulating against him. His mouth burst from hers on an expletive, then buried into her hair, just above an ear.

'Slow down, baby,' he muttered, his breathing hot and heavy. 'Slow down.'

'No,' she cried, desperate in her desire. 'No, I don't want to slow down. I want you. Oh, please, Val. Please…'

'Sorry, honey,' he groaned.

He wrenched himself right away from her, and her arms dropped back to her sides like lost souls with no place to go. *She* was a lost soul, somewhere out there in limbo. No, not limbo. Hell. She was in hell.

She stared up at him through pained eyes. 'Why did you stop?'

'Why do you think?' he grated out, raking his hands back through his hair.

'I don't *want* to think,' she moaned.

'I can see that. Hell, I can see a whole lot of things now. You need a man badly, honey. A lot of men would have already taken complete advantage of that fact. But I'm not *that* much of a bastard.'

'No,' she choked out, shaking her head. 'No. You don't understand. I don't want just *any* man, Val. I want you. Only you.'

He sucked in sharply. 'Only *me*?'

She nodded, her tongue thick in her mouth. 'No man has ever made me feel what you made me feel today,' she said huskily.

'You certainly didn't show it,' he said, half-admiring, half-accusing.

'Why do you think I agreed to come out with you tonight, despite knowing your reputation with women?'

'Is my reputation with women all that bad?'

'It is in my eyes. You're a playboy, Val. And play-boys are not my favourite species of male. You treat women like toys. When you get bored with one you simply go get yourself a new one.'

'That's a very cynical view, Lucille.'

'I'm a very cynical woman.'

'Yes, I'm beginning to see that too. That ex of yours must have done a right number on you. But that's no excuse for you lumping all men together and distrusting every single one of them.'

'I don't. Just a certain type of man.'

'And I'm that certain type of man?'

'Yes.'

'You think I treat women like toys?'

'Yes.'

'Well, I beg to differ. I treat women very well. Hell, I *love* women. I think they leave men for dead in every regard. They're nicer, and more honest. They're better company, better conversationalists, better damned everything, in my opinion. I'd rather spend an evening with a woman than a man any day.'

Lucille's smile was wry. 'I don't doubt it, Val. But any attractive woman would do. We're not really individuals to you. Just temporary and very dispensable playmates.'

'Which suits you just fine on this occasion, doesn't it?'

She stiffened under his merciless black gaze, struggling again with her pride and her conscience. But to no avail. She was too far gone for a change of mind now.

'Yes,' she bit out. 'All I want is for you to make love to me.'

He shook his head. 'Oh, no, honey. *Love* hasn't anything to do with what you want me to do to you.'

She squirmed under his brutal honesty till resentment took over. Who was he to judge her, this man who'd probably had more tacky one-night stands than she'd had doughnuts?

'Okay,' she said, and used words he couldn't possibly mock. Or misunderstand.

But, having expressed herself so crudely, she totally spoilt everything by blushing.

He stared at her with glittering black eyes. 'Well, that shouldn't be too hard, honey. I've been wanting to do *that* since I first saw you at Erica's place. But we do have one problem. I actually don't carry protection with me on *just* dinner dates. What do you suggest we do about that?'

Her chin lifted in defiance of his ongoing attempts to embarrass or intimidate her. 'I do have some condoms.'

His eyebrows arched. 'I thought you said you'd never done this before.'

She gritted her teeth. 'I bought a box when I was going to paint the town red after my divorce. They're still intact in the bathroom drawer.'

'How many?'

'I don't know. Half a dozen, I think.'

'That'll have to do, I guess,' he said, his hands lifting to begin undoing the buttons on his shirt.

Lucille stared at him, then at the strip of darkly tanned skin which was rapidly unfolding.

She swallowed when he ripped the shirt off and tossed it aside.

'Like what you see, honey?' he drawled, his fingers already on his belt.

He had a lovely shape: broad shoulders tapering down to a narrow waist and equally narrow hips. He looked very fit, his stomach flat and hard, well-defined muscles rippling over his ribs and up his arms. Dark curls matted the middle of his chest but didn't hide his small male nipples, which were startlingly erect.

She stared at them, then up at his glittering black eyes. She didn't know if he was aroused. Or angry. Or both.

Frankly, she didn't care, as long as he did what she wanted. Suddenly she was without shame, compelled by the fiercely urgent desire to put her hands on his naked flesh and to feel his on hers.

'Yes,' she rasped. 'Yes, I like what I see.'

'Then go get the condoms, honey,' he ordered. 'We only have all night.'

CHAPTER SEVEN

'I'M SO glad you could get off early this afternoon to come shopping with me,' Michele trilled as she searched one of the size eight racks in the boutique. 'You're usually too busy on a Friday. Come on. Help me look, Lucille. Don't just stand there, daydreaming. I simply have to have a new dress. Tyler's parents are throwing a pre-wedding party for his sister and her fiancé tomorrow night and they've already seen me in every party dress I own.'

Lucille suppressed a sigh and tried to put her mind to helping Michele find something. But her heart wasn't in it. Her heart hadn't been in anything all week. Not since…

Oh, God, she couldn't bear to think about it again. The humiliation on that Tuesday morning when she *had* woken up and found Val Seymour's head on the pillow next to her. Then the shame of remembering everything she'd done with him into the wee small hours of the morning. Was there any position he *hadn't* coerced her into trying? Though coercion was probably the wrong word. She'd been more than willing. Only sheer exhaustion on both their parts had eventually stopped the sexual marathon.

She'd wanted to flee before he woke up, but how could she? It had been *her place. Her bed.* And *her* decision to *go* to bed with him.

In the end she'd brazened it out, waking him with

a mug of steaming coffee and asking him politely if he could possibly get up and go home as she had to shortly leave for work. Before he could say a single word, she had thanked him for his understanding in giving her some privacy and not contacting her ever again.

She would never forget the way he'd looked at her at that moment. The shock in his eyes. And then the anger.

He'd tried arguing with her, insisting he wanted to see her again. But she'd stayed firm, knowing that to see him again would put her on the rocky road to ruin. She was not about to become addicted to having sex with an incorrigible womaniser, no matter how worthy of addiction his brand of sex was. In the end he'd done what she'd asked and left, banging the door loudly behind him.

But his being out of sight had not put him out of her mind. How could it when so many places and things around her apartment reminded her of him— not just the bed? He'd been a very imaginative lover, not confining their sexual activities to the bedroom. The kitchen counter had been the site of a very interesting encounter. And, naturally, the shower. Still, it had been the empty box of condoms sitting on the bedside chest that was the most brutal reminder. Lucille hadn't known a man could make love so many times in one night.

But he had. Oh, yes…he had.

And she'd wallowed in every glorious time.

'What do you think of this one? Do you think this colour suits me?'

Lucille dragged her thoughts away from that night

and back to her friend, who was holding out a slinky lolly-pink little number which would show off her slender figure and look great against her dark brown hair.

'Perfect,' she said, forming an O with her finger and thumb. 'But go try it on,' she added sensibly. 'Make sure it fits.'

It did. Just.

'You look wicked,' Lucille complimented her, and her friend smiled, brown eyes sparkling.

'Do you think Tyler will like it?'

'He won't be able to wait to get it off. That is…*if* he can get it off. It looks like it's glued on.'

Michele laughed. 'Not to worry. Tyler will peel it off with his teeth if he has to. He's a master at undressing me.'

Lucille wished she hadn't said that. Val had been more than a master at undressing her, turning the procedure into the longest and most exquisite erotic torture she'd ever known. During the time it had taken him to strip her properly she'd actually come, a sharply frantic little release he'd brought about with knowing fingers but which hadn't satisfied her in the slightest, just left her panting for more.

It was the *more* she was having trouble forgetting. Especially that first powerful penetration, which had catapulted her straight away into another, far more shattering climax from which she hadn't really recovered. Val had kept her turned on with his hands and his mouth, never letting her come down from that highly sensitised state where every nerve-ending balanced on a razor's edge. Whilst *his* flesh rested between times, *hers* stayed on red alert, hot and wet, screaming to be filled once more. And she had screamed once: the last time, when her ecstasy had been mixed with agony.

Even after all that she hadn't found any real physical peace. Her nipples had stayed painfully erect the following day. As for the rest of her…that had ached and throbbed for a good two days, another reason why she hadn't been able to put the wretched man out of her mind.

Once or twice yesterday she'd been tempted to ring him, actually looking up his number in her files and jotting it down in her notebook. But she hadn't. Her pride wouldn't let her. She couldn't bear him looking at her with real contempt in his eyes.

With a bit of luck, the restlessness and frustration which had started escalating again on Wednesday would go away soon. Not that it showed any signs of abating. She hadn't slept well the last couple of nights and was beginning to feel distracted at work, her mind drifting to things sexual without any reason.

Thankfully, this wasn't a busy time of the year for relocating people. Not many firms would send valued employees and their families to the other side of the world in the months leading up to Christmas.

Which was why she'd been able to get time off this afternoon. A definite lull had hit Move Smooth.

'That dress over there would look fantastic on you, Lucille.'

'What? Which one?'

'The one on the mannequin in the corner.'

Lucille looked. It was red. A full-length crêpe sheath with short sleeves and a wide off-the-shoulder neckline, edged in gold guipure lace. Already an eye-catching colour and style, it had an even more eye-catching slit up one side, right to the top of the thigh.

Maybe it was the way her mind was working at that moment, or the long flowing black wig worn by the mannequin, but she immediately thought of Flame in that dress. It had the tango written all over it.

'I think it's a bit flashy for me,' Lucille said, wishing she hadn't thought of Flame. Or Angela. Or whatever the stupid woman was called. Any female who wanted *Max* Seymour over his son had to be insane!

'Rubbish,' Michele pooh-poohed. 'You have exactly the right figure to bring that dress to life. And just think of the shoes you could wear with it,' she added with a wicked little laugh.

Lucille did indeed have a sinfully strappy gold pair which would be perfect.

'But where on earth would I wear it?' she sighed.

'What about your boss's Christmas bash? Everyone will be done up to the nines in that crowd. And what better colour for a Christmas party than red? Oh, go on, Lucille. Try it on.'

Lucille glanced at the price tag first. 'It's an Orsini,' she stated drily. 'And far too expensive.'

'No, it's not. I'm buying it for you.'

'You are *not*!'

'Yes, I am. *You* gave *me* an Orsini dress not all that long ago.'

'Yes, but I bought it on sale and it didn't fit me any more.'

'That's irrelevant. You gave it to me without a second thought, and I'm going to give you this one in return. Now, don't argue, Lucille. I have the money. Tyler gives me a monthly allowance that I couldn't spend if I tried.' Without further ado she called the salesgirl over and had her hang the dress in one of the changing rooms.

Lucille gave in gracefully and went to try it on.

She had to confess the red dress looked pretty spectacular, though it wouldn't have wanted to be any tighter. Lucille frowned as she twisted and turned to inspect the back as well as the front.

The front wasn't too bad. Her D-cup breasts weren't too disgracefully exposed. But she groaned at the lower back view. There, the dress hugged her backside like a plaster mould, making it look like a ripe peach, a very *large* ripe peach. She really would have to stop devouring custard cream doughnuts at every turn. Somehow, since Monday night, the compulsion to continuously satisfy her sweet tooth had become savage, resulting in an extra inch at least on her hips. Soon it would be goodbye size ten and hello size twelve!

Not that Val would mind, came the sudden and sneakily corrupting thought. He had simply *adored* her womanly body. Hadn't been able to get enough of it. Lavished compliments over the lushness of her breasts, the softness of her stomach and the well-rounded globes of her bottom.

'I'm getting fat,' she'd moaned when he'd first finally got her naked and she had caught a glimpse of herself in the cheval mirror standing in the corner of her bedroom.

'Honey, you're nowhere near fat,' he'd reassured her. 'Your figure's fantastic. Most women these days are too thin. Men like a bit of flesh to get hold of. Did you know it's a measure of status for men in some of the poorer countries to have plump wives? It proves they've got the money to feed them. Lush curves are considered very sexy. And they're sooo right...'

As he'd said all this he'd turned her to face the cheval mirror, and had held her there while he ran his knowing hands all over her body, kneading her breasts and stroking her stomach, her thighs, the area between her thighs, making her feel beautiful and adored and so sexy it had been criminal.

'Oh, Lucille!' Michele exclaimed on opening the dressing-room door. 'It's just you! I knew it would be. What a pity you don't have a man to wear it for.'

Lucille couldn't help thinking it was a pity too. She would have liked to wear it for Val. She would have liked to wear nothing for him again as well.

She grimaced at this last thought. God, she was hopeless.

'Still, if you go somewhere wearing that dress,' Michele added wryly, 'you won't be manless for long. They'll be jumping out of the woodwork and onto your beautiful bones.'

The high-pitched ring of Lucille's cellphone brought a welcome halt to *that* little conversation.

'I hope that's not your office,' Michele said as Lucille fished the phone out of her handbag.

'Sure to be,' Lucille muttered before she pressed the button. Who else would be ringing her on her mobile at four o'clock on a Friday afternoon?

'Lucille Jordan,' she said in her best business voice.

'Lucille. It's Val.'

Her stomach flipped right over. Had she conjured him up simply by thinking about him? Given him a telepathic message that she was wanting him now even more than before?

'I can't get you out of my mind,' he ground out before she could gather herself enough to say a word, any word which Michele wouldn't take the wrong way. She was already giving her a curious look as if to say *Who is it?*

'Oh, yes, Mr Valentino,' Lucille said briskly, using the first name she could think of. 'How may I help you? Wasn't everything to your satisfaction the other day?'

His momentary silence at the other end was telling. But then he laughed. 'So that's how it is, is it? You're with someone and you can't talk. Or you *won't* talk, more like it. You won't even use my name, though it actually *is* my name. Val's short for Valentino. Named after the great lover himself. I'll bet you didn't know that.'

'No, I didn't,' she said stiffly, though it was damned appropriate.

'At least you haven't hung up,' he remarked drily, 'so that's a start. To answer your question, everything was more than satisfactory the other day. I told you, passion always gets me in, and you're one passionate woman, Lucille. More than passionate. You're... incandescent...when you're turned on. That's why I find I can't leave things at a one-night stand. I have to have more of you, my darling. Do you like me calling you my darling?'

Oh, God, he had no idea. It sent quivers running up and down her spine. It made her melt inside. It made her glow all over.

Was that what he meant by incandescent?

She quickly turned her face away from Michele's curious eyes so that she wouldn't see anything as telling as rosy cheeks.

'*I* sure as hell do,' he went on. 'Especially when the ice princess can't slap me down or tell me to shut you. You have to stay polite and say the right things. So say the right thing, my darling Lucille, and tell me you'll be with me tonight. Here. At my place this time. If you don't, I might just have to come and camp outside your building. I might even bring a guitar and serenade you like the lovesick swains of old. Would you like that?'

Lucille gulped down the lump in her throat. What did you say to such a man? The hide of him. The magnificent hide!

'I *know* you still want me,' he continued, his voice low and seductive. 'I can feel it in your silence. I can hear it in your breathing.'

'I'm sorry, Mr Valentino, but—'

'I'm well aware you don't want to be seen in public with such a notorious playboy,' he broke in, his tone sardonic. 'But I'm not asking for that, am I? This will be a very private rendezvous. We'll eat in. I'll have dinner delivered. I'll have *everything* delivered. We'll spend the night drinking champagne and lolling around in the spa and having the most glorious sex. What more could you possibly want? No one will know. I'll be your secret toyboy and you can be my secret playmate. So what do you say to that, my darling Lucille? Have you got the courage to take some more of what you want? Or don't you dare?'

Daring her was almost as good as calling her his

darling. A surge of adrenaline shot through her veins, bringing with it a heady recklessness.

'I do apologise, Mr Valentino,' she said matter-of-factly, thrilling at her ability to sound so cool in the face of the mad excitement fizzing through her blood-stream. 'But I simply can't drop everything at the moment. I'm very busy. And I never drive into the city area during peak hour. But I'll pop over later this evening with everything you want. Shall we say...eight? Would that be satisfactory?'

She wasn't sure what his silence meant this time. Surprise, perhaps, at the ease of his success? Hopefully nothing like smug triumph. She could bear anything but that.

'You won't regret it,' he said at last, his voice low and vibrating with the most seductive passion.

It got to her. Just as *her* passion got to him.

But it was still only sex.

She had to never forget that.

For the first time since meeting Val, Lucille began to worry that she might.

'I already do,' she muttered under her breath as she clicked off the phone.

When she looked up it was to find Michele frowning at her. 'This Mr Valentino's a client, I presume?'

'Yes. I settled him into a fancy apartment in Darling Harbour on Monday afternoon.'

'What on earth does he want that you have to drive over there personally on a Friday evening?'

Lucille reckoned she deserved an Academy Award for not blushing. 'Move Smooth always provide their overseas clients with brochures which tell them all the best tourist spots and restaurants, plus the pitfalls of the Australian language and culture,' she said, quite truthfully. 'Anyway, I forgot them on Monday. It was a bit of a rush job. I promised to drop them in for him this week and haven't yet, and he's a bit peeved. So I'd better do it, or he might complain to the big boss. He's by way of being an old friend of hers.'

'How old?'

Lucille thought it was time to terminate this line of questioning. 'For pity's sake, Michele, you're not trying to play matchmaker again, are you?'

'It was just that he has an Italian name and we already decided you might go for a foreign guy. You don't fancy this Mr Valentino at all?'

'He's the last man on earth I'd consider having a relationship with,' she stated firmly. Have sex with, yes. But a relationship? No.

'Too old?'

'It's not a question of age.'

'Too ugly?'

'He's not at all ugly.'

'What, then? Not even a single teensy-weensy spark?'

'No.' It was more like fireworks. 'Trust me on this.'

'Mmm. If you say so. But don't think I'm going to give up altogether. I'm determined to find you a man-friend by Christmas. Just think, wouldn't it be great to take a really good-looking guy home with you on Christmas Day and give your family a nice surprise?'

Lucille tried to picture what would happen if she showed up at the typically suburban family barbecue on Christmas Day with Val Seymour on her arm.

It was too impossible a scenario to speculate over, and since it was never going to happen, why bother?

What *was* going to happen was she was going to go over to Val's snazzy apartment this evening, where Val was going to shag her silly all night. And then, by morning, with a bit of luck, she might have got him out of her system. And vice versa.

But he wasn't out of her system yet, she accepted, her hand trembling as she dropped the phone back into her bag. Not by a long shot. 'I'd better get this dress off and get going, Michele,' she said, trying not to unravel just yet. 'I'll have to drop back into the office and collect the brochures before Jody locks up for the weekend.'

What she was really going to do was get out of here and go home. She simply could not keep sounding normal when everything inside herself had gone haywire.

'You're just trying to get out of my buying you this dress,' Michele said. 'But it isn't going to work. I'll just pay for it after you've gone and give it to you on Monday, at lunch.'

Lucille threw her a resigned smile. 'If you must.'

'I must.'

'You're a sweetie, Michele,' Lucille said, kissing her on the cheek. 'Thanks.'

'Just promise me you'll wear it somewhere before Christmas.'

'I promise.'

'I aim to keep you to that.'

'Bye, Michele. Have a good weekend.'

'You too. And don't do anything I wouldn't do.'

Too late, Lucille groaned to herself as she hurried out of the boutique. I already have.

CHAPTER EIGHT

FIVE to eight that evening found Lucille alighting from a taxi outside Val's exclusive apartment building. She'd been just too nervous to drive. Too…distracted.

Not that she *looked* nervous. The reflection she glimpsed in the revolving glass door as she pushed her way into the lobby was that of a confident, well-groomed business woman. The tailored black suit she was wearing was smart rather than sexy, although the skirt *was* pretty tight and short, as was the fashion these days, and the lapelled jacket *was* nipped in at the waist, highlighting her hourglass shape. Her make-up was subtle, her blonde hair swept back into an elegant but severe French pleat. The only jewellery she wore was her plain gold wristwatch.

Admittedly, the addition of sheer black stockings and black patent stilettos gave her overall appearance an edge which might suggest that their wearer was on her way to something other than a business appointment.

Lucille had been tempted to wear something seriously sexy, but she worried Val might talk her into staying the whole night, and she didn't want to leave the building the next morning in something totally unsuitable for daywear. The last thing she wanted was to waltz out of his apartment *looking* like a woman who'd been out on the tiles all night, so to speak.

As Lucille approached the reception desk in the

lobby she hoped the black leather briefcase she was carrying would complete the businesslike façade she was adopting. After all, no one would know that it contained nothing but the basic essentials for feminine survival, including a spare pair of black panties and a new packet of pantyhose to replace the skintight teddy and stay-up stockings she was wearing underneath her suit if needs be.

The man behind the desk looked up at her approach. He was about forty, with thinning brown hair and sharp grey eyes which seemed to see all at a glance. He had a tag pinned to the breast pocket of his navy blazer which introduced him as the 'Night Manager'.

'Good evening, ma'am,' he said in nasal voice. 'How may I help you?'

'Mr Seymour in 12A is expecting me,' she replied, her crisp, no-nonsense tone belying the butterflies which were playing catch-me-if-you-can in her stomach.

'I'll have to ring and check, ma'am. Your name, please?' He produced a handkerchief and wiped his nose.

'Lucille Jordan from Move Smooth.' Lucille hoped that adding a business name would deflect any possible suspicion on the man's part that she was really a call-girl in disguise. It was unfortunate that she couldn't just walk over to the lift and ride up to Val's floor unannounced. But the lift wouldn't work without a keycard pass.

The night manager spoke to Val on the telephone in hushed words, and Lucille imagined that his unctuous smile had a slightly knowing quality as he hung up and turned back to her. 'Here's your temporary pass for the lift, Ms Jordan. Could you please drop it back here at the desk when you eventually leave? If I'm not here personally, then someone else will be. I go off duty at four.'

'Thank you,' she said stiffly, not happy with the implication that he didn't expect her to leave till practically dawn. What *had* Val said to him?

She never found out. Val distracted her from her intention to ask by opening his door as she walked towards it. His gaze raked over her from head to toe, taking in everything on view, especially the shoes and the briefcase.

A mixture of pride and defiance had her giving as good as she got, though her facial expression was challenging rather than drily amused.

He wasn't wearing black this time. He was wearing grey. Dark grey trousers and a pale grey shirt, open at the neck. His hair was still wet from a shower, but his face was again sporting a few days' growth.

She actually liked the designer stubble look on him. It was devilishly sexy.

So was his smile. 'And what are you selling tonight, Ms Jordan?' he drawled, black eyes sparkling.

His teasing irked her for a moment, till she realised this was the only way to play this game. Start taking it all too seriously and she'd never be able to cope. Erica had spelled it out for her. Men like Val were fun. Fun to be with. Fun to sleep with.

She had to learn to go with the flow.

'I was hoping to interest you in a new type of personal protection,' she said without batting an eye.

His eyebrows arched. 'Door to door salespeople are certainly much better-looking than they used to be. Do come in, Ms Jordan. I'll be interested in hearing your spiel. Or do you prefer to demonstrate your products?'

'Oh, no,' she said with a perfect poker face. 'We ice princesses don't demonstrate. We just like to talk.'

Their eyes met, hers throwing all kinds of challenges at him.

Suddenly, his hand shot out and he yanked her inside, kicking the door shut behind her. The briefcase clattered to the tiled floor as he pushed her up against the door and crashed his mouth down on hers, his lips prying hers apart and his tongue darting deep.

Lucille might have gasped at his oral assault if she'd been capable of gasping. But her mouth was too full of him for anything but a low, whimpering moan.

Soon, it wasn't just his tongue she had to contend with. There were his hands, those sensual, knowing hands which had taken so long to undress her the other night.

They weren't slow tonight. They had her jacket off in no time. Then the straps of her black satin teddy were pushed off her shoulders and pulled down her arms till she was naked to the waist, the satin straps left to dangle by her elbows, imprisoning her arms by her sides.

All this with his mouth still on hers, seducing her into a state of utter submission to his will.

His abrupt lifting of his head startled her back to the raw reality of her standing there like that, half-naked, her back against his front door.

She could have done something about it, she supposed. Could have somehow wriggled the straps back up onto her shoulders. They weren't all that tight around her elbows.

But she didn't, of course. The truth was she liked being on display for him. It was exciting to pretend she couldn't move to cover her bared breasts, that she was somehow a helpless captive of his male aggression.

She loved the way he was looking at her, his eyes narrowed and smouldering. Her head began whirling with her own dark desires, the sexual tension she'd been suffering from all week soaring to new heights. If he didn't do something soon, she thought, she'd go mad!

He did. He touched her. His right hand reaching out to graze the backs of his fingers across her aching nipples. She groaned and willed him to do it again. He did, watching her eyes dilate and her breathing quicken.

'Oh,' she gasped when he cradled both her breasts in his hands at once, moaning when he began rubbing over the now rock-hard tips with his thumbs.

'Stop,' she choked out when everything began spinning out of control inside her head. 'Stop...'

'But you like it,' he insisted. 'You want me to touch them, lick them, suck them.'

'Oh,' she moaned when he bent to do just that.

'Don't stop *now*,' she groaned when he suddenly straightened.

His eyes searched hers. Hot, blazing black eyes.

She met them with her own glazed green ones.

'Please, Val,' she whispered shakily. 'Please...'

The next few moments happened in a flash. One second she was sagging back against the door, her arms limp by her sides, the next she was leaning over a nearby marble console, gripping its corners with nerveless hands and staring, wide-eyed, into the mirror on the wall.

Val was behind her, his hands frantic on her clothes. Her skirt was being hitched up, the teddy unsnapped at her groin, her body being made accessible to his.

Her eyes widened at the realisation of what he was going to do. But not a word of protest came from her lips. Because this was what she wanted too. Him, inside her. Just like this. Every muscle and nerve-ending she owned was already tightening in anticipation of his penetration.

His stopping long enough to protect them both amazed her. She moaned when she finally felt his flesh pushing into hers, then again when he began pumping into her, his hands gripping her hips like twin vices. His impassioned thrusts sent her body rocking back and forth, her hot, hard nipples rubbing against the cold, hard marble.

Lucille had never felt the like, either in her body or in her head. Watching herself in the mirror seemed to add to her rapture as she revelled in her reflection's abandoned sensuality; her flushed face; her wild green eyes; her panting mouth.

It was all terribly decadent, but more exciting than anything she'd ever done!

She liked watching Val too. Liked watching the almost hypnotised way he was staring down at what he was doing. Unable to see that low in the mirror, Lucille let her heated imagination paint an erotic picture of her bared buttocks, raised and taut with tension, their pale, soft-skinned globes quivering under Val's powerful and primal rhythm.

Her insides contracted wildly at the thought, and he

cried out, grimacing as his head fell back and he came. She came too, just as suddenly, bringing a strangled moan from her widely gaping mouth. She gripped the console even harder, for fear of somehow dislodging his body from hers, a thought that didn't bear thinking about. She wanted him to stay deep inside her. No, *needed* him to stay inside her.

She sobbed when the spasms went on and on.

'It's all right, baby,' he assured her throatily. 'It's all right. Here. Don't do that.' He reached round to pry her white-knuckled fingers from the marble, then slowly, carefully, levered her upright, his hands spreading to press possessively against her stomach and breasts.

Eventually her tortured flesh calmed, and her head tipped back against his shoulder on a long, adrenaline-draining sigh.

'That feel better now?' he crooned, kissing her shoulder, her neck, her ear.

Lucille quivered under his feathery lips, amazed that he was still partially erect inside her, and even more amazed when her heartbeat began quickening again. Yet this was what he'd done the other night. No sooner had one episode ended than another would begin.

'Fantastic,' he murmured. 'Simply fantastic.' He nibbled at her earlobe, bringing another erotic little shiver. 'Do you think we might stay like this for ever? We could be bronzed into a statue. They could put it in a park somewhere. Lovers from all over the world would come to see us.' When his mouth covered her ear entirely and blew softly inside, she trembled un-controllably.

'I know that doesn't mean you're cold,' he whispered. 'I've never known a woman as hot as you are once you get going.'

'Please stop, Val,' she groaned, despite not making any physical struggles to get away from him. 'I...I don't think I could cope with anything more just now.' She was starting to *really* feel him. Which could only mean he was becoming fully erect again. Lord knows how. The man had to be a machine!

'Pity,' he muttered, then slowly, gently, eased out of her.

She flinched at his withdrawal, plus at the unexpectedly bereft feeling that washed through her, biting her tongue lest she tell him she'd changed her mind, that she wanted him back inside her, that she wanted him to make love to her till she collapsed from exhaustion.

'You do *do* things to me, darling Lucille,' he murmured, his mouth still hovering over her ear, 'that haven't been done since I was a randy twenty-year-old. Still, you're quite right to stop me for a while. There's a delicious dinner awaiting us, not to mention a bottle of Dom Perignon chilling in an ice bucket. I had seafood and salad delivered earlier, with crispy rolls, and a mango cheesecake for afterwards. But I'll need a few private moments to make myself decent before we adjourn to the dining room.

'I'll just pop in there,' he said, nodding towards the powder room which led off from the foyer. 'Meanwhile, you might like to get yourself decent again too. I don't think I could cope, sitting sedately at a table with you looking quite as...stimulating...as you do at this moment.'

He left her alone to stare at herself in the mirror once more.

Her reflection didn't bring the word 'stimulating' to mind. *Stimulated* was more like it. Her eyes were gleaming, her cheeks glowing. Her mouth was still swollen, and so were her breasts. She looked the epitome of a woman who'd been thoroughly seduced and totally corrupted. She looked wanton and wild and more than a little wicked.

Getting herself decent again, she conceded ruefully as she yanked her teddy back up—and down—into place, was impossible. She could cover her nakedness with clothes, tidy her hair and replenish her lipstick. But nothing could change what was going on inside her head.

The truth was she was in danger of becoming seriously addicted to Val's lovemaking. Though love had absolutely *nothing* to do with what he'd just done to her, as he'd pointed out the other night.

It had been raw sex. Lust, in its most primitive form. Almost animal-like, both in position and intent. There had been no deep or fine emotions involved. No special caring. No...

Lucille's harsh thoughts were interrupted by the memory of Val caring enough to stop and protect her when *she* hadn't been able to stop. It couldn't have been for himself so much. After all, he knew *she* hadn't been sleeping around with other men.

That had been a kind of caring, hadn't it?

Maybe not, she was forced to accept. He was probably so used to using protection in his promiscuous world of casual sex and musical-chair girlfriends that he did it on autopilot.

Only a fool would start thinking she might mean anything special to him. Only a fool would start imagining she was anything more to him than a novelty, to be summarily dumped once he grew bored, or someone more...incandescent...came along.

Like Flame.

The sound of a toilet flushing had Lucille scooping her jacket up from the floor and hurriedly dragging it back on. As she buttoned it up, she staunchly buttoned up any futile female feelings her thoughts had dredged out of her subconscious.

Play it cool, she told herself as she smoothed down her skirt and smoothed back her hair. He's just a male body, to be used for your own pleasure, used as he's using *your* body.

Yes. Keep *that* thought in your head and you might survive this experience relatively unscathed. At worst, you won't end up any more screwed up and cynical than you already are.

When Val emerged from the powder room she spun to face him, her chin lifting in automatic accord with her inner resolutions.

He took one look at her face and sighed. 'Oh, no, you don't. It's after dark. The ice princess has been put to bed, remember? Hell, leave you alone for a minute and all my good work has gone to waste.'

Lucille bitterly resented being referred to as some kind of project that had to be worked upon. 'Leopards don't change their spots, Val,' she snapped. 'I am what I am, just as you are what *you* are.'

'Ah, yes, I keep forgetting what a worthless, womanising bastard I am. But what does that make you, Lucille? Or daren't you think about that?'

She struggled with a stab of shame, but managed to bury it behind the cold-blooded pragmatism she'd set her course upon. 'I'm a normal woman,' she pointed out coolly. 'With normal needs. But I'm also a once-bitten-twice-shy divorcee who has no intention of putting her life—or her happiness—in the hands of a man again. That's why I tried to keep things between us to a one-night stand on Monday night. Because you're an incredibly skilled lover, Val, and I was worried I might do something stupid like fall in love with you.'

'Heaven forbid you'd do something *that* stupid,' he said testily.

'For pity's sake, I wouldn't have taken you for a man who'd be so super-sensitive. If you must know, I don't want to fall in love with *any* man, not just you. Anyway, I've had some time to think about things since last Monday, and I've realised my fears about falling in love with you were way over the top. I mean…I fancy you like mad, Val, but love is a different kettle of fish entirely. I was just a bit confused by all the great sex. I've never enjoyed making love so much before with a man whom I wasn't in love with. It took me a while to get used to the fact that I could have such strong physical feelings without love.'

'But you finally managed it?' he said drily.

Lucille refused to react to his sarcasm. 'Yes. I've finally managed it. When you rang me today, I was actually thinking about ringing you.'

Now *that* was an outright lie, but a girl had to have her pride. Couldn't have him thinking just the sound of his voice had obliterated her vow never to see him again.

'Get to the bottom line here, Lucille, if you don't mind. What is it that you want of me?'

Lucille composed herself to take the plunge. 'I want what you offered me on the phone.'

'And what was that? Please remind me. After all, that was several hours ago. A lot of water has gone under the bridge since then.'

'A strictly sexual and very private affair,' she bit out, well aware that he was trying to humiliate her for some reason. Ego, probably. He liked calling the shots where his sex life was concerned and didn't like any woman stating the terms under which he could have her.

'Ah, yes,' he drawled. 'I do recall. I'm to be your secret lover and you my secret playmate. So for how long would you envisage this...arrangement...lasting?'

For ever, came the involuntary thought.

Lucille's heart lurched. Lord, but she was even more addicted here than she'd realised.

'For as long as we both find it mutually satisfying,' she managed to say, gritting her teeth hard.

'And is this to be an exclusive arrangement?'

She blinked, then stared at him. 'You...you want to see other women at the same time as me?'

'I didn't say that. Actually, I'm overwhelmingly enamoured of *your* charms at the moment. But anything's possible, I suppose. Do *you* want the right to see other men?'

'No!' she denied, far too heatedly, before she could think better of it.

His eyes glittered, but with what emotion she couldn't be sure. Possibly anger. 'I'm flattered that you wish to be faithful to me. But I would have imagined faithfulness was out of sync with a strictly sexual affair.'

'Maybe, but I'd still rather you didn't see anyone else,' she grated out, hating the thought of him with *any* woman, but especially with that Flame female.

'Why?' he mocked. 'It can't be because you'd be jealous. Only lovers in love get jealous. Worried another woman might take some of the steam out of me, is that it? I can appreciate why. It takes quite a bit to satisfy you, once we've gotten the ice princess out of the way.'

'If you're going to insult me, Val, then I'm out of here.' As if to make the threat real, she snatched her briefcase up from the floor.

'If *I'm* going to insult *you*! Now that's a laugh. You've been doing nothing but insult me since we met.'

'I've only been honest.'

He glowered at her, then sighed. 'Yes. Yes, you've only been honest. But do you have to be so brutal? Here, give me that stupid damned thing. You're not going anywhere, except inside here with me.' He took her briefcase and tossed it in a corner again, then took her elbow and steered her into the living room and over to one of the bar stools.

'Sit,' he ordered.

Lucille sat. He was so right. She hadn't really been going anywhere.

A bottle of Dom Perignon was sitting in an ice bucket at one end of the bar, two fluted glasses at the ready. Val walked round to lift the bottle out. He wiped it with a striped teatowel and began unscrewing the top.

'Look,' he said firmly as he worked to release the cork. 'Let's stop this fruitless game of one-upmanship. I can't stand it. Honesty I don't mind, but not nastiness. Or vindictiveness. I realise you've been hurt in the past, Lucille, but *I* haven't hurt you, have I?'

'No…' she agreed, but warily. Because he would, if she let him. She just knew it.

'Surely, then, behind these closed doors at least, we can be friends as well as lovers.'

'Friends?' she echoed blankly.

His smile was wry. 'People who like each other. People who trust each other. People who are actually *nice* to each other.'

Lucille was truly taken aback. 'I…I've never been friends with a man before,' she hedged.

Now *he* was the one who was taken aback. 'Not even your husband?'

'Him least of all.'

'Then why not start with me? I make a good friend to a woman.'

'And why would that be?'

'Because I like women.'

'That *is* a good start,' she conceded, thinking what a strange turn-up for the books this was. She'd come for sex and now he was offering her friendship as well.

'I also like the things women like,' he added.

'Such as?'

'Music. Dancing. The theatre. Films. Books.' The cork popped and he poured the sparkling liquid into the crystal glasses.

'What about cars and golf and your mates?'

'I don't own a car. I can't play golf, and I have no mates, as such. I'm not much of a man's man, I'm afraid.'

'I'm never going to tell Michele any of this,' she muttered.

'Who's Michele?' he asked as he pushed her glass in front of her and began sipping from his own.

'My best friend.'

His eyebrow lifted, and so did his mouth. 'And I'm to be a secret from her as well? I find that hard to believe, knowing women as well as I do.'

'I couldn't possibly tell her about *you*. She's trying to find me a boyfriend before Christmas. She'll think you're perfect.'

'Silly Michele.'

'She's not at all silly. She's an advertising executive. And smart as anything.' Lucille took a deep swallow of the champagne. God, it was delicious. 'But she's a hopeless romantic.'

'Now that's a dreadful disease to suffer from, being a hopeless romantic.'

She eyed Val reproachfully. 'I thought you said no more remarks like that.'

He actually looked guilty. 'You're right. That was uncalled for. Please accept my apology.'

'Accepted,' she said, and smiled.

He cocked his head to one side. 'You know, you don't smile nearly often enough.'

'I haven't had much to smile about,' she said ruefully. 'Till now.'

'Wow! That sounded like a genuine compliment.'

She blinked, then smiled, a bit surprised herself. 'It was, wasn't it?'

'I'm going to drink to that. You too. Drink up, darling.'

Lucille winced at his easy use of that word. She knew it didn't mean anything, but she wished she wouldn't say it all the same. 'I'll get drunk if I drink any more on an empty stomach,' she told him.

'Does it matter?'

'I guess not. I don't have to drive home later.'

'You're planning on staying the night?' He was obviously startled.

Lucille hoped she didn't look as hot as she felt all of a sudden. 'I came in a taxi. I don't like to drive into the city alone on a Friday night.'

'Sensible. Well, stay the night anyway,' he suggested casually. 'Stay the whole weekend if you like.'

If she *liked*. Dear God...

It was a struggle to look nonchalant.

'We'll see,' she said. 'I might have to go home at some stage.'

'True,' he drawled. 'You might need some sleep before Monday.'

Their eyes met over their glasses of champagne. He smiled a slow, sexy smile, and her stomach flipped right over.

'You're a wicked man, Val Seymour,' she chided.

'And you're a wicked woman, Lucille Jordan.'

Her chin tipped up saucily. 'We're a good match, then, aren't we?'

His smile widened. 'Actually, I was just thinking the same thing myself.'

CHAPTER NINE

'YOU'RE looking extra fab for a Monday,' Michele said as she joined Lucille at their usual lunch table.

Her eyes had narrowed on Lucille's new suit, which, though quite plain in design, was a brilliant turquoise colour which looked even more brilliant in the sunshine. It also fitted like a glove, showing every curve of her curvy figure.

'Is there anything you should be telling me?' Michele asked suspiciously.

Lucille produced a face which would have convinced anyone—even the knowing and cynical Erica—that she was as pure as the driven snow. In the three short weeks since she'd met Val, she had learned to become an actress worthy of an Oscar nomination. No one would know that she was leading such a wicked double life. At work she remained Ms Jordan, super-cool consultant from Move Smooth. In her leisure hours she was Val's hot-blooded lover. Sizzling. Sensual. Sexy beyond belief.

Her heart skipped a beat just thinking about some of the things she'd done.

'Like what?' she asked, having a struggle to keep her voice and eyes ingenuously innocent.

'Like where you were all weekend, for starters. I rang once on Friday night. Twice on Saturday and at least three times on Sunday. But I never seemed to catch you in.'

'Really? Oh, well, Friday night I saw a movie, then Saturday I went shopping nearly all day. Christmas is only a few weeks away, as you know, and I like to get my present-buying in early. I'm not sure what could have happened on Sunday, though I *was* tired from all that shopping and napped quite a bit. Maybe I was asleep and didn't hear the phone. I keep the ring turned down pretty low. When was the last time you tried?'

'About nine-thirty last night.'

'Oh, well, I was definitely in bed by then.'

Technically, everything she'd said to Michele was the truth. She *had* seen a movie on the Friday night. *Titanic* on cable TV. Or she'd sort of seen it. When the heroine had taken off her clothes for the hero to paint her in the nude, Val had decided he wanted to do the same to her. Only once she was naked, and draped artistically over the sofa, he had confessed he didn't have any proper paints but would a bottle of perfumed bath oil and her make-up brush do?

The rest of the film had been a bit of a blur.

Then, on the Saturday, she *had* gone shopping all afternoon, whilst Val had been busy at a full dress rehearsal for the show. He'd sent her off with his credit card, squashing the objections she'd raised by saying she never let him spend any money on her by taking her out, so the least she could do was let him buy her a couple of sexy negligées which she could swan around the apartment in, instead of always wearing *his* dressing-gown.

So she'd come back with some very naughty Femme Fatale label lingerie and nightwear, plus the turquoise suit she was presently wearing, which she'd paid for herself.

Then, on the Sunday, she *had* spent quite a bit of time sleeping. Just not in her own bed. She'd been exhausted after Val had been positively insatiable on the Saturday night, courtesy of the Femme Fatale gear.

When he'd finally arrived home from rehearsals around seven, he'd been suitably impressed by the slinky black lace robe she'd been wearing, but totally speechless when she'd slipped it off her shoulders and revealed what was underneath. Anyone would think he'd never seen a black leather-look corset before. The kind with a built-in push-up half-cup bra from whose highly inadequate confines her voluptuous breasts had been spilling.

Lucille had every intention of buying some more Femme Fatale items in the not too distant future, if that was the effect they had on him. It was a pity that she couldn't recommend them to Michele. But how could she? How could she tell her *anything*?

Michele would be flabbergasted. And possibly quite shocked.

Lucille might have been shocked too, if she could come down to earth long enough for such feelings. At the back of her mind she knew she was on a one-way trip to disaster, but it was just too exciting a journey to stop now. She was already chronically infatuated with Val and his lovemaking. Infatuated. Addicted. Maybe even obsessed.

But, oh…what a magnificent obsession!

'What did you want me for?' she asked Michele, hoping she didn't sound too distracted. It had been a mistake to start thinking about Val and sex. Hard not too, however, when she was planning on meeting him straight after work, only a few short hours away. That was why she was wearing the showy turquoise suit. And precious little else.

'I had some news to tell you which couldn't wait till today,' Michele said.

Lucille did her best to focus on her friend, but her mind kept drifting. 'Oh? Good news, I hope.'

'Very. I'm going to have a baby.'

'A baby!' Lucille was suddenly very, very focused. 'But...but you've only been married a few weeks,' she said, frowning.

Too late, Lucille realised this wasn't the reaction Michele was hoping for.

Seeing the hurt in her friend's eyes, she did her best to make amends. 'Well, aren't you the clever couple!' she exclaimed, smiling brightly despite her instant doubts and fears. 'It takes some people years to conceive. Is Tyler pleased?'

'Thrilled to pieces.'

Lucille wished she could say the same, but she wasn't. Divorce was bad enough when there weren't any children involved. She'd give Michele and Tyler a few years at best. And now there was a baby coming. An innocent little baby...

'I had no idea you both wanted a baby so soon,' she commented as casually as she could. 'Was it an accident?'

'No, not at all. Tyler told me on our wedding night that he didn't want to wait. From my dates, I must have fallen pregnant on my honeymoon.'

'How romantic,' Lucille murmured, not too drily.

So it had all been Tyler's idea! She might have guessed.

Michele sighed dreamily. 'I think so, too. I'm so happy, Lucille, that I sometimes think it can't possibly last.'

Exactly what Lucille was thinking.

The waitress came over and they ordered their usual: ham and salad sandwiches—no onions—two cappuccinos, a low-fat blueberry muffin for Michele and a doughnut for Lucille. Custard and cream this time.

'I have some other news for you, too,' Michele went on as soon as the girl departed.

'You can't possibly know the sex of the baby yet,' Lucille protested. 'It's way too soon.'

'No, nothing to do with the baby. Harry and his heiress are getting married. What have you got to say to that?'

'I'd say that *heiress* is the optimum word in that little proposal.'

Michele shook her head. 'There you go again, being super-cynical. Just as well I wasn't a rich bitch or you'd be thinking all Tyler wanted from me was a financial merger. But no more talk about me. I want to talk about you.'

'*Me?* What about me?'

'Met any Latin lover types lately?'

'Afraid not.' Lucille hated lying, but three weeks ago didn't classify as 'lately', surely.

'Any decent-looking guy at all ask you out this last week?' Michele asked exasperatedly.

'No. Not a one.' Val didn't bother any more. He knew what her answer would be.

'I can't understand it. You must freeze them off with that attitude of yours.'

'Possibly.'

'Have you worn that red dress yet?'

'Haven't had much opportunity,' Lucille replied. 'Christmas parties don't start till December,' she added. 'And that's still two weeks off.'

Not that she intended going to any parties this year. She had better things to do than stand around all night, drinking cheap sparkling wine, eating lukewarm finger-food and trying to fend off drunken yobbos. Erica's Christmas party wouldn't be much better. The food might be hotter, the wine more expensive and the yobbos richer, but basically it would be just the same.

'Then I'll have to *make* an opportunity,' Michele insisted. 'I'll get Tyler onto finding some tickets to something you have to dress up for. Maybe something at the Opera House. An opera, or the ballet. We'll go to supper afterwards. Somewhere swanky where eligible rich men-about-town gather. And I don't want you finding some pathetic excuse not to come along. I didn't buy you that dress for it to sit in your wardrobe.'

'I will wear it. I promise.'

'You certainly will, because I'll be there to see it on you.'

'Okay, but no surprise partner for me, please.'

'I wouldn't do that to you.'

'Yes, you would.'

'Never. Blind dates are the pits, in my opinion. I'll give you a call once I know when and where, but keep this Friday night free.'

Lucille was about to make some excuse for this

Friday when she remembered it was the opening night of *Takes Two to Tango*. When Val had mentioned the première a week ago, her look had warned him not to ask her to go with him.

She could just imagine it! All the press would be there, snapping photos of them together and printing them in the weekend papers along with suitably salacious captions, after which everyone would know what had been going on. Michele. Erica. All the women at work. Possibly her own mother.

Marion Jordan wasn't an aficionado of gossip columns, but there was always some busybody neighbour who saw such interesting items and couldn't wait to relay the good news. Her mother was the kind of woman who believed 'nice girls' didn't kiss a boy on the first date, so seeing her divorced daughter linked with a man of Val's reputation would probably make her reach for the smelling salts.

Mrs Jordan had been forty-five when Lucille was born, so there was more than the usual generation gap between her and her youngest child. Lucille's two older sisters had been twenty and twenty-two at the time, so they'd been like aunts, rather than sisters. Disapproving aunts, to boot. As she'd grown up, Lucille had never been able to do a thing right in their eyes. They'd called her 'fast', which was an old-fashioned euphemism for slut.

Her mother had been more than relieved when she'd married at the relatively young age of twenty-two.

'Dear Roger' had been Lucille's saviour, in her mother's eyes. A handsomely macho man. A good provider. A potentially perfect husband and father.

Her mother had thought Lucille crazy for leaving

him. And nothing Lucille had ever said had changed her mother's mind. No doubt she also thought her disgusting daughter was now out there sleeping around indiscriminately. Her sisters certainly thought so, always making snide remarks about her morals whenever Lucille was stupid enough to attend a family function.

Lucille wondered why she was trying to protect her own reputation—plus her family's feelings—when she'd already been labelled a tramp and a fool. What difference would it really make if everyone knew about her affair with Val? Her boss certainly wouldn't hold it against her.

She supposed the bottom line was pride. Pride and her own personal survival. She had to live with herself, when all was said and done.

Lucille jumped in her chair when her mobile rang.

Her heart fluttered as she reached down into her carry-all and brought it up to her ear. It could be the office, or a client. But she knew it wasn't. That strangely telepathic sense she was developing where Val was concerned was working overtime.

'Lucille Jordan,' she answered in her best working voice.

'I simply had to talk to you,' Val pronounced frustratedly. 'I'm about to strangle everyone here. Angela is acting like some bloody prima donna. Raoul is dancing like a second-rater. The rest of the cast members aren't looking too happy, either. My director's just flounced out of here in a huff and we're only five days from opening. Talk to me, Lucille. Calm me down. You're the only one who can do that lately. I'm about to burst a boiler.'

Lucille's eyes darted to Michele, who was thankfully distracted by the waitress arriving with their food on a tray. 'I'm having lunch with someone at the moment, Val,' she whispered. 'I can't talk.'

'Damn and blast.'

'Look, give me half an hour and I'll ring you back.'

'I might be dead by then,' he growled.

'You'll survive,' she murmured, her eyes still on Michele, who was now busy chatting with the waitress about the lovely summery weather.

'I suppose you're having lunch with that friend of yours,' he grumped, clearly not wanting to get off the line. 'Michele. You told me you did that every Monday.'

'*Did* I?'

Lucille's surprised retort sent Michele's dark eyes snapping back over to her.

The waitress took the hint, and left.

'Don't you remember?' Val purred, all temperament forgotten as his sexual predator personality took over.

'No, I don't.' Lucille voice was cool. It had to be. Michele was looking straight at her.

'You tell me all sorts of interesting little things when we're in bed together. I know more about you than you realise.'

'Such as?' She was still sounding cool, even whilst she was heating up inside.

Michele's interest finally fell to her food.

'I know you're the youngest in your family by far. I know you've got two older sisters whom you don't relate to any better than your elderly parents. I know you started work as a receptionist at a real estate agency straight out of school, then moved on to sales a few years ago by sheer accident when none of the sales staff turned up one weekend and you sold three houses. I know you hated school, liked boys from an early age, and were a bit of a rebel. I know you lost your virginity at sixteen in the back seat of a car and actually enjoyed the experience. I know you adore doughnuts. I know you read just about anything but prefer thrillers, both in books and movies. I know you're mad about men with large...er...egos.'

She laughed. She couldn't help it.

Michele raised her eyebrows at her over her coffee cup.

'I really *have* to go, Jody,' she said, and Val chuckled.

'So I'm Jody now, am I? What happened to Mr Valentino?'

'My coffee's getting cold...'

'Can't say the same for myself, all of a sudden. Don't worry about ringing me back again. I know you're busy. You've done the trick, anyway. I'm considerably calmer. At least, my mind is. My body's another matter. I'll go back inside and read this lot the Riot Act. As for that pathetic director. He's out. I'll direct the damned show myself.'

'Are you sure that's a good idea? Shouldn't you just try to smooth his ruffled feathers?'

'Yeah. You're probably right. I'm far too hot-headed for my own good sometimes. It's all that Latin blood in me. It never knows when to lie down and die.'

'I know what you mean,' she said drily.

'Wicked girl. Just wait till you get here tonight. By then, I'm going to be desperate.'

She wanted to whisper *How desperate?* in a provocative fashion, but didn't dare. Michele was listening to every word.

'Must go,' she said curtly. 'See you later.'

'Don't you dare be late,' he called out just before she clicked off.

She threw Michele an apologetic glance as she popped the phone away and picked up a packet of sugar for her coffee. 'Sorry about that. A bit of an emergency at the office. Jody didn't know what to do. A disgruntled client.'

'Not Mr Valentino again!'

'Afraid so. Some people,' Lucille sighed with a brilliant poker face, 'are just never satisfied, no matter how hard you try to please them.'

The more sex I have, the less I want. But not with you, my darling. With you, the more I have, the more I want. His hand stopped its teasing, featherlike kisses at her earlobe.' And further.

CHAPTER TEN

'IT WAS right what I told Michele,' Lucille said thickly when Val started running tantalising fingertips up and down her spine. 'About some people never being satisfied.'

Val had just returned to where she was still lying face-down on the thick blue rug in front of the imitation marble fireplace. Her lovely new turquoise suit was somewhere between there and the front door. So were the Femme Fatale white satin thong and matching half-cup bra, which hadn't rated a second glance, so intent had Val been on getting her naked.

When he'd said he'd be desperate by the time she arrived, he'd really meant desperate. He'd already been naked under his robe when he'd let her in, stripping her without preamble then sweeping her up into his arms. She'd thought he was going to carry her to his bed, but he hadn't made it past the sofa facing the fireplace. He'd been so impassioned that they'd fallen off onto the rug.

Of all Val's lovemaking, this had been his most urgent, his own climax stunning in its intensity. Yet here he was, less than a minute back from the bathroom, touching her again, wanting more.

And she…she was so hopeless at resisting him.

'I just can't seem to get enough of you,' he murmured, his voice and fingertips incredibly soft and sensual. 'Usually it works the other way around with me.

The more sex I have, the less I want. But not with you, my darling. With you, the more I have, the more I want.' His mouth replaced his fingertips, feathering kisses all the way down her spine. And further.

Lucille was glad her head was buried in the plush pile, her face flushing with the deliciously shameful intimacies his tongue was inflicting upon her. Her mind began squirming but her body exploded with pleasure. She even liked the feel of his stubbly chin rasping against the soft skin of her inner thighs. In the end, nothing he did to her felt wrong, or embarrassing. By the time he rolled her over and slipped a big sofa cushion under her head she would have done anything he asked. When he straddled her body and presented himself at her lips, she didn't hesitate. She kissed the velvet tip, cupping him with her soft woman's hands and drawing him deep into the warm, wet well of her mouth.

'Oh, God, Lucille,' he groaned, shuddering with pleasure. 'Lucille…'

Her name echoed in the room as he rocked back and forth on his knees, his raw cries of rapture moving her in a way which should have been a warning. But Lucille was too carried away to appreciate the emotions gathering within her. Her own sexual excitement was still too intense, masking the depth of her feelings, giving her a deceptively cold-blooded excuse for doing what she was doing.

Lust. That was all this was. Lust.

She didn't stop to think that lust was usually a selfish creature. Greedy and needy and utterly self-absorbed. It didn't seek to give, rather than receive. It didn't care for another's pleasure, only its own.

Lucille's hands were tellingly soft on his flesh, her mouth selfless and sweet. All she could think of was satisfying *him*. Pleasing *him*.

When Val groaned a warning groan and went to withdraw, as he'd always done before, she would have none of it, her hands keeping his straining flesh firmly captive whilst her eyes flashed fire up at him.

His face betrayed an agony of indecision. He wanted to. She could see it in his eyes, feel it in his tensely held flesh. Lucille knew he wouldn't need much persuading.

She began to move her hands, and her head.

The most glorious feeling ripped through her when she saw his eyes shut and heard his moan of sheer surrender. Was it elation she felt? Triumph? Power? What? What was this force which was compelling her to do what she'd never liked in the past? Why was she finding such pleasure in *his* pleasure? Why didn't she care if she came or not?

This wasn't what she'd wanted to be, she agonised for a split second. A woman who gave without receiving, a woman who let her body be used for another's mindless satisfaction, a woman who didn't demand the respect and consideration she rightfully deserved.

Yet, to be honest, this didn't feel anything like that. She didn't feel like some kind of victim, or slave. She felt wonderful. She felt incredible. She felt…good.

He shouted her name once more, then his head tipped back in ecstasy.

She was standing out on the balcony, leaning on the railing and watching the multicoloured lights of the

Casino winking in the darkening waters below, when Val came out with two glasses of chilled Chablis. The sun hadn't long set but already the night was upon them.

'Thanks,' she said absently as he handed her one, her mind elsewhere.

'What's wrong?' he asked softly.

She glanced over at him. He was wearing navy silk pyjama pants and nothing else. She'd dressed fully again, and quite quickly, saying that she couldn't stay late again or she'd be useless at work in the morning.

'Nothing's wrong,' she lied.

'Yes, there is,' he insisted. 'Tell me.'

Her mind raced to find something to tell him, anything but the truth—that she wasn't sure she was as cut out for this...arrangement...as she'd thought she was, that she was afraid she was becoming emotionally involved with him. Or worse. After all she'd promised to herself, and all she'd claimed to everyone about playboys and what she thought of them. Especially Michele.

Michele! That was it! That was what she could tell Val. And it wasn't a lie, either. She *was* worried about Michele.

'If you really must know,' Lucille said edgily, 'I'm worried about Michele. She told me today that she's pregnant.'

Val looked perplexed. 'Why is that a worry? She's married, isn't she? To Tyler Garrison, the Rags to Riches publisher.'

'And heir to the Garrison media fortune,' Lucille added tartly, gulping down a massive mouthful of wine. 'How long do you think *that* marriage will last?'

'I have no idea,' he said calmly. 'I'm not a prophet.'

'I'll give it five years at best.'

'I presume you think he doesn't really love her?'

Lucille's laugh carried true scorn. 'Oh, come now, Val. Men like Tyler Garrison marry for lots of reasons, but rarely love.'

'Is that so? What do they marry for, then? I'm curious to know what you think.' He was watching her with annoyingly intense eyes, as if she was a specimen to be examined.

'Ego, mostly. And sexual convenience. Money, sometimes, I'd imagine.'

'Would you care to elaborate?'

'They either marry rich bitches, to boost their financial reserves. Or supermodels, to boost their egos whilst bonking them silly.'

'And which was your Michele? Rich bitch or supermodel?'

'Neither. Which brings me to the only possible reason for Tyler marrying her. An heir.'

'Ah. Yes, of course. An heir. Not a child, of course. Or a baby. An heir.'

'You're making fun of me.'

'No, no, I don't think anything you've just said is at all funny. I think it's terribly sad.'

Her shoulders squared. 'Life *is* sad, Val. And so are some marriages.'

'I think yours must have been.'

'I'm not talking about *my* marriage.'

'Aren't you? I think you are. I think everything you've just said has something to do with your marriage.'

'Then you're wrong. My marriage had nothing in

common with Michele's. I didn't marry a rich man. I married a very ordinary man. A plumber, to be exact.'

'His being a plumber has nothing to do with anything.'

'Then what has, Mr Psychoanalyst? You tell me, since you know everything about me, even things I haven't told you. Things I haven't told anyone!'

'Your husband didn't love you.'

Lucille's eyes widened and she just stared at him.

'He didn't love you. Or care about you. Or understand you. Or appreciate you. He took the beautiful, brave, brilliant girl that you must have been and tried to crush her under his chauvinistic male ego.'

Lucille's mouth had dropped open. Tears threatened and she had to battle for control, shoring up her defences again as she always did. With sarcasm and cynicism.

'My mother would be surprised to hear that. Dear Roger was a prince in her eyes. I was a feminist bitch who wanted the world and wouldn't do what a good wife should do without complaint or question. I wouldn't even have a baby.'

'I don't believe that. If you wouldn't have your husband's baby, then it had something to do with him, and not you. I think you'd make a marvellous mother.'

Lucille could feel her chin begin to wobble. She tipped the rest of the wine down her throat and prayed for calm.

But all calm had been shattered. She was beginning to shake inside. 'I really don't want to talk about this,' she bit out.

'But you need to, Lucille,' Val challenged. 'Can't you see that? It's poisoning you. Everything you say and do is influenced by what happened in your marriage. It's twisted your views and warped your mind. You can't even have a normal relationship with a man because of it.'

'Are you saying our relationship isn't normal?'

'It's way from being normal, and you know it. But normal *is* what I want with you, Lucille. I'm sick of all this secret coming and going. I'm sick of your being ashamed of my being your lover. I'm not ashamed of you. I want to shout our relationship from the rooftops. I'm not a bad man, Lucille. Your ex-husband's the bad man. He's the one who deserves to be judged, not me. So let's do that now. Let's judge him together. Then let's get him the hell out of your life!'

Lucille was thrown into turmoil by Val's impassioned tirade. She hadn't realised he felt so negatively about their arrangement. She'd thought he'd be more than happy to go along with a strictly sexual affair. A lot of men would have been.

His desire to have a real relationship with her stirred deeply female longings which would not be denied. Because underneath that was what she wanted too, despite all her supposed lack of faith in men. As for his idea of their judging Roger together... That was fraught with far more personal and emotional risk than Val realised.

She hadn't visited that place in her memory in a long, long time. Not directly. Or in detail.

On top of that, how could she explain everything Roger had done, and *hadn't* done, without sounding as self-pitying and selfish as her own family had accused her of being?

She didn't want Val looking at her and thinking the same things.

Still, she had to try, didn't she?

It was time.

But as she tried to gather her thoughts and her words, Lucille found that deciding and doing were two entirely different things.

'I...I don't know where to begin,' she choked out.

'Anywhere. What's the worst thing he did to you that you can think of? The thing you can never forgive? The thing that's still eating into you, even now?'

'The baby,' she blurted out, and he looked shocked.

'What baby?'

'Our baby,' Lucille confessed with a shudder, shutting her eyes in a vain attempt to shut out the pain of remembering.

'You had a *baby* with your husband?' He sounded stunned.

'She...she was stillborn at six months. Right on my twenty-eighth birthday.'

'Oh, God, Lucille. I'm so sorry.'

Lucille eyes snapped back open, blazing with bitterness and anger. 'Roger wasn't,' she ground out. 'He wasn't sorry at all. He hated my being pregnant. He hated my feeling sick all the time. He hated the house being messy, hated the meals he missed out on, hated me not being able to jump up and get him a beer whenever he wanted one. But he especially hated not getting any sex. The doctor said we weren't to do anything, you see. I'd had some spotting. The night I went into labour, he...he insisted. It was either that or he was going to go out and get himself laid elsewhere, by a *real woman*.'

Lucille closed her eyes and shook her head. 'He cheated on me anyway, after I'd lost the baby. It was all for nothing. My whole marriage had all been for nothing. Roger hadn't wanted a partner. He'd just wanted a convenient lay and a free housekeeper. His agreeing to a baby had just been a ploy to stop me from leaving him. He never wanted a child for himself, or for us.'

'I don't think I need to know any more,' Val said sadly.

'Oh, no, you haven't heard nearly enough yet. Do you know what we did practically every weekend of the six years I was married to him?' Now that she'd starting talking, she simply couldn't stop.

'Tell me.'

'*We* didn't do anything. Roger played golf or cards with his mates. Or drank beer and tinkered with whatever new car he'd bought with *his* money. Which, of course, meant the money I earnt as well, because *my* money was *his* money. Oh, yes, he did give me some sex every Friday and Saturday night, before he went to sleep, but nothing like the kind of sex he'd lavished on me during our courtship days and our honeymoon. There was precious little foreplay. Nothing of romance. Mostly he just pounded away till he came. If I hadn't by then, it was my bad luck, because afterwards he just rolled over and went to sleep. When I complained, he said he couldn't help it if I'd become frigid. He said his mates had told him that once you were married the sex was never as good, and he could see what they meant.'

'Why in God's name did you marry him?'

She laughed. 'Why? you ask. Why does any woman

marry a man? Because I *loved* him,' she said sneeringly. 'Or I loved the man he seemed to be when I first met him. The man who couldn't do enough for me, who couldn't keep his hands off me, who flattered me and complimented and wooed me till his ring was on my finger.'

'How old were you when you married him?'

'Twenty-two.'

'That is young. Still…you shouldn't have stayed with him, Lucille. You should have left him long before the baby.'

'It's easy to say that, but a lot harder to do it.' She stopped to suck in some much needed air, and to try to calm down a little. 'The bottom line is I was afraid to leave.'

Val looked aghast. 'He hit you?'

'No.' Lucille shook her head. 'No, he didn't actually hit me. But he was big man, with a big voice. He used to shout me down all the time. If I dared complain, or ask him to do anything around the house, he called me a whingeing, nagging woman who didn't know when she was best off. So, yes, I *was* afraid of him, in a way. But I think what kept me with him all that time was my fear of telling my mother that I was unhappy in my marriage and that I wanted out.'

'But surely your mother would not have wanted you to stay in an unhappy marriage.'

Lucille tried explaining. 'Mum's never hidden the fact I was always a disappointment to her. Always getting into trouble at school. Always going around with unsuitable boys. When I brought Roger home, she changed her tune. She thought he was just the ant's pants. Of course, he was a very good-looking man.

And older than my usual boyfriends. He also had his own plumbing business. A big plus in both my parents' eyes.'

'Didn't they ever see you were miserable with him?'

'If they did, they pretended not to. Admittedly, Roger put on a pretty good act around them. He'd be all lovey-dovey, with his arms always around me. He was the jealous type, was Roger. He never let me out of his sight. To begin with, marrying him made me feel good. In the end, it made me more miserable than I could ever describe. I kept telling myself things would get better when we had a baby. But of course that was just wishful thinking. His attitude during my pregnancy, then after the baby died, really made me wake up to himself. It was then I started working up the courage to leave him and make a life for myself.'

'How did he take your leaving him?'

'The stupid man actually seemed shocked. Yet I hadn't slept with him after the baby died. Not once. I just couldn't. I moved into the guest room and he got himself a girlfriend. Or two. Frankly, the man should never have married me at all. You're right. He never really loved me. He did lust after me in the beginning. Maybe in his poor pathetic mind he thought that was love. After we got married, he often used to say how great it was to have sex without using a condom, and without having to spend any money on me first.'

'Selfish bastard. So he made a fuss when you left?'

'You should have seen the turn he put on in front of my parents. Went crying to them and saying he'd tried everything to please me. Accused me of being one of those feminist types who wanted the man of the house to do the washing-up and such. He also said I wanted to control all the money, which was a laugh. By then I'd simply taken control of the money I earned. But the *coup de grâce* was when he said he wanted to try for another baby and I wouldn't. As if I'd ever have had another baby with that bastard.'

'I don't blame you.'

Lucille was moved that he understood.

'What I do blame you for, however,' Val added sternly, before she got too carried away with his kindness, 'is letting one man spoil the rest of your life. Because of him, you stopped believing in love. And you stopped trusting men, especially men like me. I know life can be cruel, and some men are mongrels, but there are mongrels in all walks of life, Lucille. Sure, I have a bit of a reputation as a ladies' man. And, yes, some of it has been earned. But if you're honest you must see the media have a field-day with the supposedly playboy type. There's as much fiction as fact in what they report. And what fact there is, is given a highly salacious slant. That's how they sell their stories. You shouldn't presume someone is bad without getting to know them first. You shouldn't prejudge on rumour and gossip. You should wait and see. Then make your assessment.'

Lucille heard the sense in what he was saying. But habits did die hard, and it was difficult to throw off cynicism just like that, and embrace the future with such a clean and possibly naïve slate.

What was in it for him, she speculated warily, if she began thinking the way he wanted her to think? If she began trusting men again?

'I don't want to get hurt,' she said carefully.

'Who does?'

'I won't be any man's slave.'

'I would hate that, anyway. I love your independence, and your spirit. I even love the occasional glimpses of the ice princess. She's such a delicious challenge.'

Her green eyes slanted instant wariness at him. 'Is that all I am to you, Val? A challenge?'

'Amongst other things.'

'What other things?' she demanded to know.

He smiled. 'Ah, now it would be very foolish of me to put all my cards on the table at once.'

She stiffened. 'I warn you, Val. Don't play games with me.'

'Isn't that what you've been doing with me? Playing games?'

Her insides tightened. 'I wouldn't put it quite like that.'

'Well, I would,' he countered. 'And, whilst it's been fun, I want more than just sex from you now, Lucille. I want you to be by my side in public as well as in bed. And I want you to be proud of that fact. I'm a good catch, honey, not some sleaze-bag gigolo who has to be kept your dark little secret.'

'But I'm not trying to catch you,' she flung at him, irritated by his calling her honey, and perhaps by his making her feel guilty.

'Don't you think I know that? But not every relationship has to end in marriage. I want to see you on a more regular basis. I want take you out places. I'd like to go away for weekends together. Or perhaps even live together.'

'*Live* together?'

'Yes. Would you like that?'

'I thought you were going overseas in four months' time,' she pointed out drily, trying not to panic. Because she was so tempted to say yes, despite all her immediate doubts and qualms.

'That was three weeks ago. Things have changed since then.'

'You've made things up with your father?'

'No.'

'Then what's changed?'

'For Pete's sake, Lucille, stop playing dumb and give me an answer. Yes or no to living together.'

Playing dumb? She wasn't playing dumb. She probably *was* dumb, since he thought she should know what he was talking about. Possibly he meant he hadn't known three weeks ago what a great lay she was. Perhaps he thought if she moved in with him he'd get more of what he'd just enjoyed on a daily basis!

'It's way too soon for anything as serious as that,' she said stiffly.

His smile was wry. 'Fair enough. It was only a suggestion. It would save all those taxi fares and the time taken running back and forth across the bridge.'

'I'm sorry that seeing me is so inconvenient.'

'So am I. But I guess that's the price I have to pay for the pleasure of your company. But it's your *company* I'll be wanting more of in future, Lucille, not just your body. And not just here, in this apartment.'

Lucille still couldn't come to terms with their relationship going public. 'And what if I say no to that idea as well, for the time being?' If he cared for her at all, if he understood what she'd just told him, then surely he would give her some more time.

'Then, sadly, I will have to say no to any more of this…arrangement…you've been enjoying.'

'I don't believe you'd do that,' she said, flustered and shocked by his stand. 'No man would give up what I've been giving you.'

His face hardened. 'This man would.'

Panic coursed through her veins, as did a swift anger. Did she mean so little to him that he could jettison her from his life simply because she wouldn't do things his way?

Apparently so.

The hurt was intense, but so was her resentment.

'So that's it, is it?' she snapped. 'Get lost, Lucille. Simply because I won't play the game by your new rules. After all the things I just told you. All those private and personal details. My God, I was right about you all along. You fooled me with your Latin lover charm and your ''I love women'' line, but underneath you're just another male chauvinist pig, with no real understanding of anything but what *you* want. To think that I…I—'

She broke off just in time, squashing her rising hysteria and dredging up her best ice princess act with the remnants of her pride. Her green eyes were glacial as they raked over him.

'Sorry, lover. If that was a poker bluff, then you just lost. I'm outta here. And I won't be back.'

Spinning on her heels, she brushed past him and stalked back through the open sliding glass door into the living room. There, she dumped her empty wine glass on the grey granite bar-top, scooped up her bag from where she'd dropped it earlier and marched to the front door.

There, she hesitated for a second, but when there were no sounds of his coming after her she wrenched it open and left, banging it loudly behind her.

The man on the balcony flinched at the sound, lifted his glass to his lips and drained it dry.

'Bravo, Val,' he said bitterly. 'Bravo.'

CHAPTER ELEVEN

LUCILLE refused to cry. She held onto her self-righteous fury the whole time she waited for the night manager to call her a taxi, and again during the fifteen-minute drive home. She flounced out of the taxi, still feeling outraged, propelling herself across the pavement and up the steps towards the building's security doors.

She didn't see the dishevelled lout lurking in the outer shadows of the portico, and wasn't at all ready for the push and grab attack on her handbag. One second she was stabbing her key angrily into the lock; the next she was sent flying, and her bag was being wrenched off her shoulder. Instinctively, and perhaps stupidly, she tried holding onto it, but the drug-crazed youth was way too strong for her and she had to let go, or have her shoulder pulled out of its socket.

He ran off, leaving her sprawled on the ground, not really hurt but in a state of shock. Dazed, Lucille glanced around, her mouth already opened, ready to shout for help. But there wasn't anyone in sight. The street was deserted and there was no one going in or out of the building. Yet it wasn't all that late.

Clearly Monday night was the perfect night to mug someone, Lucille thought ruefully as she struggled to her feet. No witnesses. No passing Prince Charming to chase after the bastard and tackle him to the ground.

No Good Samaritan to take her arm and check if she was okay.

Thankfully, her set of keys was still in the door, so she at least had the means of getting into the building and her flat.

But she groaned at the thought of everything else that had been in her handbag. All her bank cards and credit cards. Her Medicare card. Her driver's licence. And over fifty dollars in cash.

Her phone was ringing as she let herself with suddenly trembling hands into her flat.

Lucille hurried to answer, grateful to have someone to tell her horrible experience to. It was probably Michele. Or maybe her mother. She hadn't rung for a while. For once, Lucille wouldn't mind it being her mother.

She sank down on the chair next to the hall table and picked up the receiver, but before she could utter a single shaky word Val's voice came urgently down the line.

'Thank God, you're home at last. I've been going out of mind, calling myself all sorts of names, hating myself even more than you could possibly hate me. You're right. I was a presumptuous pig and an arrogant fool to think you could just forget everything rotten that had happened to you in five minutes simply because I said to. Lord knows, I understand how the past can screw up your mind and your emotions. I wasn't being rational. There again, I haven't been all that rational ever since I met you, Lucille. I know you won't believe me if I tell you I love you, that I fell in love with you that very first night we spent together. But it's true. I know I rushed you tonight. I know it.

But I thought... I hoped... Hell, I've turned into a blithering idiot.

'For pity's sake, tell me you feel something for me other than a sexual attraction. If not, just tell me I can see you again. Under whatever terms you want. Geez, I'm making a right mess of this. Max would be appalled. He always taught me that women liked their men to be suave and masterful. But to hell with that. I don't feel in any way suave or masterful tonight. I haven't ever since you walked out.'

His outburst had dazed Lucille. Stunned her, in fact. Delayed shock from the incident downstairs had already dried her throat and sent her palms all clammy. Her head started spinning.

'Val,' she said weakly, her spare hand clutching at her temple. She could almost feel the blood draining away from her head. 'I...I need you.'

He groaned. 'You don't have to say any more. That's enough. Being needed is enough.'

'No, no, you don't understand,' she croaked.

'What don't I understand?' There was confusion in his voice.

'I...I've just been mugged.'

A gasp, then a frantic, 'Are you all right?'

'Yes. No. I mean...he didn't bash me. He just pushed me over. But I feel funny. I think I'm going to faint.'

'Put your head down between your knees,' he commanded. 'Fast.'

She did what he said.

'Have you done that?'

'Yes,' she answered tremulously.

'Now stay like that for a minute or two. When you

feel well enough, go and lie down. After a while, if you think you can safely stand, make yourself a cup of tea or coffee, with plenty of sugar in it. I'll be there as soon as I can. Okay?'

She swallowed. 'Val...?'

'Yes, Lucille?'

'Please don't be long.'

He wasn't long. And yet he was far too long. She had too much time to lie there and think about what he'd said, to feel her own answering female feelings well up inside her. By the time he arrived her heart and mind were in turmoil, wanting to tell him that she loved him too, but far too afraid to do so. She'd once put her life in the hands of a man who'd said he loved her, and whom she'd thought *she* loved. And lived to regret it. What did she know of this man, really, other than what he'd chosen to show her?

At the same time as Lucille was thinking these fear-filled thoughts, a voice inside her head kept telling her not to do what Val had accused of her doing; not to spoil the future because of the past; not to throw away the chance of happiness simply because she'd once been hurt.

But wouldn't it be foolish to throw all caution to the winds and rush into a relationship she might later regret? If she hadn't learnt something from her marriage to Roger, then it *had* all been for nothing.

By the time she let Val into her flat, her emotional anguish was at fever pitch. So were her twin dilemmas. To tell or not to tell. To trust or not to trust.

On top of that were her ongoing physical reactions to what had just happened to her downstairs.

'Thank you for coming so quickly,' she said tautly,

her hands clasped tightly together in front of her. 'I...I don't know why I still feel so shaken up. It's not that he hurt me or anything. But my hands keep shaking. When I tried to make myself a cup of tea just now I spilled everything all over the place. And I want to cry all the time.' Her eyes flooded with tears. 'See? There I go again.'

'It's all right,' he soothed, gathering her gently into his arms and cradling her head against his shoulder. 'You're in shock. And I didn't help by loading all my lovesick outpourings on you. I do apologise.'

Lucille gulped down her sobs and drew back to stare up into his face. He looked almost as dreadful as she felt, with dark rings under bleak black eyes.

'There's nothing for you to apologise over,' she managed, moved by his distress. Maybe he *did* love her. 'What you said...was...was...'

'Embarrassing for you,' he finished firmly. 'I understand. Truly. I can see I was deluded in hoping you might feel the same way about me as I do about you. I guess it was the way you made love to me tonight. I thought... Oh, what the hell does it matter what I thought? Passion is often mistaken for something else. I know that. You were never anything but honest with me. I'm the fool for imagining there was more. But that's not important right now. What important is the here and now of your wellbeing. Are you sure you're all right? No cuts or bruises? No sprained muscles?'

She shook her head, biting her bottom lip to stop herself from blurting out that he hadn't been mistaken. She *had* been making love to him tonight. It hadn't just been lust.

But it was still too soon for her to lay her heart bare

like that. She simply could not risk being wrong again. She'd survived the experience the first time. But only just. A second time would totally destroy her.

'I've called the police,' he said. 'They'll be along shortly. I presume you lost everything you had in your bag? Your purse, licence, et cetera?'

'Yes. Everything but my keys, which I guess is something. At least I can drive my car to work tomorrow.' The thought of going to work in the morning sent a shiver running down her spine. She hugged herself, suddenly feeling cold and clammy again.

'You're not in a fit state to go to work in the morning.'

'Perhaps I'll have the day off,' she agreed, appalled as tears filled her eyes again.

'You need the rest of the week off. And some medication as well.'

'Whatever for?' Lucille had never been one to turn to pills to survive. The doctor had wanted to put her on antidepressants after her baby died, but she'd refused. She'd needed to feel the pain. Needed to use it to face the truth, then escape a marriage which had become intolerable.

'You need something to calm you down. And to make you sleep. You've got yourself into a state, Lucille. I know of a good doctor. I'll arrange a home visit.'

'Doctors don't make home visits any more,' she scoffed.

'This one will. She's by way of being a friend of mine.'

'*She?*'

'No. Not one of my zillion ex-lovers,' he said drily.

'Just a long-time female friend. We met when she'd just left school and was in difficult financial circumstances. I found her various evening and weekend jobs in the shows my father produced so she could work her way through med-school.'

'Saint Valentino,' she murmured, not at all mockingly.

His face still became grim. 'Hardly. Ten years ago, I was driving a car which knocked her father down and killed him. Okay, so the man was drunk, and he staggered out from the kerb without warning. But I was going over the speed limit. I might have been able to swerve and miss him if I'd been going a little slower. But there weren't any witnesses to say so, and naturally I wasn't about to tell that kind of truth. What twenty-three-old with his life ahead of him would? Nothing would have been served by my going to jail, anyway. But I still felt rotten when I saw his distraught wife and daughter at the inquest. I felt even worse when they came up to me and hugged me afterwards, and said it wasn't my fault. Guilt just ate me alive till I looked them up again to see how they were. Naturally, with the father in the family having been a long-term alcoholic, they had very little in a material sense. No home. No car. Nothing. Whereas I...I was living in the lap of luxury.'

Lucille was moved by the cracking in Val's voice.

'Do you think they would take any of my money?' he went on with a wry smile. 'Not on your life. "Thank you, but we'll get by," Jane's mother said, with such quiet dignity. But I wasn't having any of that. I needed to do something. Anyway, I took Jane out for coffee and wormed out of her that she wanted to be a doctor. As I said, she'd just left school. But she was going to give up her dream to go out to work to support her mother, who wasn't well. I talked her into trying to do both, then made sure she got paid top dollar for the jobs she did for Seymour Productions.'

Val's sigh carried a wealth of feeling. 'Jane's mother died while she was an intern, a couple of years back. God, I felt so sorry for her at the funeral. Now, I thought, she doesn't have anyone. But she told me not to be sad, that her mother was where she wanted to be, with the man she'd always loved, despite everything. She then told me some cheering news. She'd met someone, another doctor at the hospital where she was working. She said she was going to marry him but he didn't know it yet. I didn't like to dampen her natural optimism by saying he might not feel the same way. And it's just as well I didn't. She's going to marry him next year. She says she's going to name her first son after me. I didn't like to disillusion her by saying I might not be worthy.'

'Oh, Val…' Lucille's tears were back, streaming down her face. What a sad, sweet story. What a wonderful woman this Jane was. And what a miserable coward *she* was.

Val looked concerned. 'You see? You're a mess, and not in a fit state to be alone. After the police have been, you're coming home with me, and I won't hear any silly arguments. I have a couple of very nice guest-rooms, as you well know. You're welcome to one of them for a while. And before you say anything, this is me being your friend, Lucille, not your recently discarded lover trying to con his way back into your good books.'

'I didn't want to...to discard you,' she sobbed. 'I just wanted things...to go on...as they were...for a while longer...'

'We won't discuss that now. We'll discuss that when you feel better. In a few days, perhaps. Things will be calmer and clearer by then. Meanwhile, I want you to lie down here on this sofa and I'll go and make that cup of tea. And if the police aren't here by then, I'll ring them back and find out where the hell they are and how long it's going to take them to get their butts into gear.'

He wasn't suave and masterful, as his father had deemed a man should be, Lucille thought as she watched him take charge. He was strong and masterful, this man who loved her.

But why does he love *me*? she wondered rather dazedly. What did he see in me that first day beyond surface beauty?

She couldn't fathom that one out. She'd been cold and cynical, as well as prejudiced and prickly. Not to mention downright insulting. So what was it which had captured his heart?

The more she thought about that, the more she worried that maybe *he* was the one who was mistaking sexual attraction for something else. He himself had told her that passion always got him in. Maybe she was the first woman to show him the sort of passion he coveted. Maybe it wasn't the real Lucille he loved at all, but the totally turned on, carried away, do-anything Lucille she became in his arms.

The thought churned her stomach, but she refused to turn her mind away from it. She had to face it, had to be sure before she dared declare anything of her own love for him. She believed Val *believed* he loved her. But love had many faces, some of them just an illusion.

So she remained silent as he went about impressing her with his caring and efficiency. He made her a mug of sweet tea. Handled the police's questions when they arrived. Rang the various numbers to cancel her credit cards. Even packed some clothes under her slightly bemused direction before she stepped in and finished it herself. He then drove her in her car over to his place, proving that he drove as well as he did everything else.

He parked in his own private parking spot, which he'd never used, then insisted on carrying everything upstairs for her—'everything' being a not-that-small suitcase and a roomy overnight bag. Like a typical woman, she hadn't known what to bring and had ended up packing far too much.

But how was she to know in advance what she might need?

Lucille was grateful to ride up to Val's floor from the basement car park, bypassing the lobby and the night manager's ongoing curiosity over her comings and goings. He never said anything but his face spoke volumes. Lord knows what he would have made of her arriving with luggage.

It would never surprise Lucille if men in his position tipped off gossip columnists with scandalous tit-bits about the residents they were supposed to serve. Val wasn't the only famous man-about-town to inhabit this particular apartment block. A well-known American tennis player had rented one of the apartments for the summer, and a billionaire bachelor businessman from

England owned the multimillion-dollar penthouse. Journalists would pay good money for scoops on either of *those* fellows' love-lives.

There again, maybe the night manager valued his job too much to risk losing it by being a muck-raker's tout. She hoped so.

'Which guest-room would you like?' Val asked as he kicked the door shut behind him, his hands full of her things. 'You can have the bedroom next to mine. Or the one opposite mine. Either way,' he said, 'you're within calling-out distance.'

'Meaning what?' Lucille asked a bit sharply, and Val's face filled with frustration.

'Meaning I'll hear you if you call out to me in the night,' he bit out through clenched teeth. 'Some people have nightmares after the sort of experience you had tonight. Post-traumatic stress.'

'I don't think I'm that bad, Val. Neither do I think I need a doctor. I feel a lot better already. Truly.'

'You might think you do now. But later on you might change your mind. I'm still going to call Jane. She can prescribe you a mild sedative, make sure you sleep at least.'

'I'm sure your Jane's got better things to do than be called out in the middle of the night to give silly women sedatives.'

'Maybe, but this is *my* call, Lucille, not yours. Now,' he said, his face brooking no more argument, 'which bedroom?'

CHAPTER TWELVE

SHE chose the bedroom opposite his, for no other reason than it was the first she came to. It was a spacious but simply furnished room, rather like those found in good hotels, with pale blue carpet, grey walls, white woodwork and grey-lacquered furniture, and no cluttering knick-knacks on any surfaces.

A single painting hung above the queen-sized bed: a cool seascape which was in harmony with the blue, swirling patterned quilt. The nearby window had matching curtains, which were drawn at that moment. The lamps on the white bedside chests were pewter-based, with pale blue shades the same colour as the carpet.

It would be a soothing room to sleep in, Lucille thought. And to wake up in.

Val lifted her two pieces of luggage onto the grey-lacquered ottoman at the foot of the bed whilst she walked over and sat down on the side. She still felt weak, and still close to tears all the time.

'I'll give Jane a ring straight away,' Val said, on glancing worriedly at her, 'then get you something to eat. If my memory serves me correctly, you haven't had much in the way of food this evening. But first, I think a nice relaxing bath is in order.' He strode over to open the door which led into the three-way bathroom. 'I know you don't think you're hurt, but you must have some bruising. By morning you'll be aching all over.'

He disappeared into the bathroom, and presently she heard taps running and steam came wafting through the open doorway.

Her frown reflected her feelings. 'You don't have to wait on me like this, Val,' she said when he came back into the bedroom. 'I'm not an invalid.'

'I know that,' he returned. 'I want to. It pleases me.'

It had pleased Roger too, she thought unhappily as Val left the room, to dance attention on her when they'd first met, and even during their engagement, though to a lesser degree. But once the honeymoon was over, things had been very different indeed. He'd been hard pushed to get out of a doorway for her. Getting her a drink or a meal, even when she was sick, had been out of the question.

How long, she wondered, would Val's kindness last? Till she did what he wanted and maybe moved in with him? Or could he afford to continue being Prince Charming because it was only a passing role? It would end in four months' time, after all.

Lucille groaned at her own thoughts. She was beginning to hate her chronic cynicism. Why couldn't she be like this Jane woman? Always full of optimism, no matter what rotten things life threw at her.

Val popped his head in the bedroom door. 'Jane's on her way. She'll be about half an hour. So get your gear off and pop yourself into that bath, madam. Or do you want me to come and do that for you as well?' he added with a dry smile.

She stood up straight away. 'I can manage.'

'I thought that might get you moving.' And he disappeared again.

Twenty minutes later, Lucille had bathed and dressed herself in a her favourite navy nightie and robe, a birthday present from her mother which surprisingly she liked. The silky nightie had narrow straps and a scooped lace-edged neckline onto which the rest was gathered, falling in soft silky folds to just below her knees. The wrap-around robe had elbow-length sleeves and a sash.

Both were cool and comfy, but hardly seduction material. With all make-up removed from her face, and her hair brushed out like a schoolgirl's, she was far removed from the well-groomed, sleekly polished image she'd always presented to Val.

Yet when she emerged from the still steaming room at the same time as Val walked in with a tray his eyes revealed he still found her highly attractive.

Not that he leered. Val never leered. He just let his gaze linger slightly on various places as they swept over her.

Her mouth. Her breasts. Her bare feet.

Lucille had never thought of bare feet as being objects of sexual desire before. But she found her naked toes squirming in the thick pile of the carpet.

His eyes finally lifted back to her face.

'You're looking much better. Find any bruises?' He walked over and slid the tray onto the nearest bedside chest, pushing the lamp to the back to make room.

'A couple on my right thigh and hip,' she admitted. 'And, no, don't ask to see them,' she added in sudden panic at the thought of lifting her clothes up for his far too knowing eyes.

She wasn't wearing panties. There again, she never wore panties to bed. But she didn't want him thinking she wasn't wearing any for him. He'd promised just to be her friend for the next few days and that was what she wanted, though whether she was testing him or herself, she wasn't sure.

'I wasn't going to,' he returned calmly. 'Now, I haven't made you anything heavy. Just a toasted ham and tomato sandwich with some hot chocolate and a slice of carrot cake for afters. I'd have brought you a doughnut, knowing how much you like them, but I don't have any. I'll get a dozen in tomorrow, and freeze them to be at the ready.'

'You don't have to,' she said swiftly. 'I can survive without doughnuts. It would probably do me good not to have any for a while, anyway. I might lose a few pounds.'

'Don't you dare. I like you the way you are.'

Lucille had almost had enough of his compliments and considerations. 'Is that my friend speaking, or my recently discarded lover trying to worm his way back into my good books?'

His shrug carried no offence at her suspicious tone. 'It's simply the truth. I adore your lush shape. I can't stand skinny women.'

'I'm far from skinny, Val.'

'Good.'

The doorbell ringing put paid to that conversation.

'Get into bed and get stuck into that sandwich,' Val ordered. 'I'll go let Jane in and tell her what happened before I bring her in to you. That should give you a couple of minutes.'

Nervous apprehension in the pit of Lucille's stomach dispensed with her appetite and she literally had to force the sandwich down. The carrot cake was left, along with most of the hot chocolate. Val scowled at both when he brought the doctor in, but he didn't say anything, for which she was grateful. He left after introductions were made, closing the door quietly behind him.

Jane was a surprise. Tall, with very short straight brown hair, she looked older than the late twenties she had to be, with one of those large-boned faces which often improved with age. On first glance she wasn't a woman most men would look at twice, but her looks grew on you very quickly. Lucille imagined that by forty she'd be very handsome. She had even features and fine grey eyes which held a serenity Lucille envied. She also had a wonderfully natural bedside manner.

'Val's told me what happened,' she said, dropping her doctor's bag on the floor and perching on the side of the bed. When she crossed her legs, Lucille noted they were very good legs. She probably had a very good figure too, under that rather severe grey suit she was wearing.

'Beastly world this is sometimes,' she added, 'but at least you weren't seriously hurt. The poor fellow who robbed you was probably a drug addict. You have to feel sorry for them. They get so desperate.'

Lucille didn't feel sorry for him at all. But this woman did. Val was right. She was a rare human being.

'Val said you had some bruises but you wouldn't show him. Could I see them, please?'

'Of course.' Lucille pushed down the bedclothes and hitched up her nightie, turning over onto her side.

Jane's touch was gentle. 'Mmm, they're nasty-looking, all right, but nothing to worry about. I'll give you the name of a cream you can buy to rub in and get rid of the bruising more quickly. You might develop a few aches and pains by morning as well, but nothing a couple of baths and a good painkiller can't put right. I'll just take your blood pressure,' she said, and bent down for her bag.

She frowned on taking it. 'One-sixty over eighty. The top figure's a bit high. You're not afraid of me, are you?' she asked, smiling wryly.

'Not at all,' Lucille denied sharply.

'Then Val's probably right. The incident has upset you more than you realise. You're wound up, tight as a drum. Your blood pressure isn't dangerous but you need to relax. Would you like an injection? Or maybe some sleeping tablets?'

'I'd rather not have either,' she replied tautly.

'Why's that?'

'My mother got on the merry-go-round of sleeping tablets and never got off. I can cope. Honestly I can. And it's not just tonight's incident which has me in a bit of a bind at the moment. It's…well…I guess you could call it…life.'

'Or maybe you should call it Val,' Jane said on an unexpectedly dry note, her intelligent eyes gauging Lucille's reaction to her intuitive guess. 'You're in love with him, aren't you? And he's got you into such a state you can't think straight.'

Lucille saw no point in denying it. 'You might say that,' she said, and sighed a shaky sigh.

'The man's a menace. Oh, don't get me wrong. He's a lovely human being. Kind as the day is long. And surprisingly decent, despite that decadent father of his. He just doesn't realise the effect he has on women. I had a terrible crush on him for years. It was awful. Did he ever tell you how and when we met?'

Lucille nodded.

'In that case you can understand how vulnerable I was all those years ago. Just a baby at eighteen. And here was this gorgeous and rather exotic creature, caring about me and my mother, being incredibly kind in getting me jobs, then paying me far too much for them. Thankfully, I had enough sense to hide my feelings. Even back then I knew loving him was futile. Dashing young bucks like Val didn't fall in love with plain girls like me. Eventually, I got over my romantic fantasies and became his friend instead, which is a far better relationship to have with him, I assure you. Being his girlfriend would be hell, in my opinion. He's too much man, if you know what I mean. Too driven. Too passionate. Too…intense. Only a woman of like mind and like nature could keep up with him, or keep his interest. That's why his girlfriends never last. I've no doubt that one day he'll fall in love, but heaven help the woman if she doesn't love him back.'

Lucille knew exactly what Jane meant. But was *she* the woman he loved? Or just the woman he wanted at the moment? Why did that Angela female keep popping into her head?

'Val told me that you and he are just close friends,' Jane went on thoughtfully. 'You haven't told him you love him, have you?' she added worriedly, peering into Lucille's strained face.

'No...'

'Good. If you *want* him to fall in love with you, that would be the kiss of death.'

'He...he says he's already in love with me,' Lucille said tentatively.

'He is? My goodness, the sneaky devil. He never said a word. But that's wonderful! Or is it? What's the problem, Lucille? Why are you keeping Mum about *your* feelings? Is it that he won't marry you, the naughty man?'

'He hasn't mentioned marriage yet. Though we haven't known each other long enough for that kind of talk. It's just that I'm having a lot of doubts...about Val's feelings for me. Or should I say about his ability to sustain them.'

'Oh, no, don't doubt that. If Val loves you, then it'll be the for ever kind. Trust me on that.'

Lucille couldn't get past the word *if*, but she thought she'd said enough already. 'Um...Val might not have wanted me to tell you about this, so don't say anything to him when you go out, will you?'

'Not a word. But do let me know when he asks you to marry him. Because if he loves you, then he will.'

There was that horrible word *if* again.

'But back to why Val called me. You're probably right about the sleeping pills. If you can do without, so much the better. But please don't hesitate to call me again if things worsen. Don't ever be too proud— or too silly—to think you can't go through life without needing any help, be that either medication or simply counselling. We all need help sometimes. Now, I'll just jot down the name of that cream for your bruises.'

She riffled through her bag and brought out a prescription pad and pen. 'I'll give it to Val and he can ring an all-night chemist and have it delivered tonight, if he so desires. And he probably will.'

'Then don't give it to him,' Lucille insisted. 'Give it to me. I'll get it tomorrow some time.'

'Good idea. When Val decides he's going to play Good Samaritan, he does it to the nth degree. And there's no stopping him. In some ways it can get a bit tiring. He simply won't take no for an answer.'

'No is a word men like Val don't understand,' Lucille muttered drily.

'I know exactly what you mean,' Jane agreed. 'They take it as a challenge and won't stop till they find some way to get their own way. But you obviously know that already. Here's the name of the cream, and a cer- tificate giving you the rest of the week off. If you're not going to take any tablets, then I think it wise you don't put any added stress on yourself for a few days. That way you'll allow Mother Nature to do the relax- ing for you. Pardon me for saying this, but might you not be better sleeping in Val's bed? Sex is a wonderful relaxant.'

'We're having a bit of a break from that,' Lucille said stiffly, and Jane's eyebrows arched.

'Mmm. A girl who can say no to Val Seymour's body? Maybe he's met his match after all. Lovely to meet you, Lucille. Take care.'

Lucille lay there after Jane left, thinking. She faintly heard the front door open and close, heralding the woman's departure. Thirty seconds later, Val knocked, then walked in.

Lucille's eyes washed over him, some of Jane's words springing back into her mind. *He just doesn't realise the effect he has on women.* Followed by the surprised *A girl who can say no to Val Seymour's body?*

It wasn't just his looks which attracted her now, though they were breathtaking enough. There was also that irresistible mixture of tenderness and passion which he infused into everything he did.

'Jane said you refused to take any medication,' he grumped, clearly unhappy with her decision.

'That's right. I don't need it.'

'Stubborn,' he muttered. 'That's what you are.'

'It's my decision, Val.'

He scowled down at the tray as he picked it up. 'You didn't eat your cake or drink your hot chocolate, either.'

'I'm sorry, I just…couldn't.'

His sigh sounded weary. 'I can see you're going to be a difficult patient.'

'I'm not a patient, Val. I'm not sick.'

'You've had a shock.'

'All I need is a good night's sleep.'

'Will you be able to sleep?'

'I don't see why not.'

'Lucky you,' he muttered under his breath. 'I'll say goodnight, then. See you in the morning,' he bit out, and whirled away from her.

She almost called out to him as he carried the tray from the room, but she bit her tongue just in time. More of Jane's words came back to haunt her, especially the ones about how men like Val were challenged by the word, *no*, then pulled out all stops to get their own way. Which was what, exactly, in her case?

He wanted her to be his girlfriend, to move in with him, to be at his beck and call in every facet of his life, both social and personal. When she'd refused, he'd pursued her on the phone then unexpectedly declared his love for her. Was that declaration real, or just a ploy to get her to do what he wanted? And what of this Florence Nightingale act? Was that a ploy, too?

Lucille groaned and snapped off the bedside lamp, plunging the room into darkness. But her head just whirled and whirled. Time dragged by and still no sleep came. Impossible, with all the mental toing and froing going on in her mind.

Lord, she was never going to get to sleep.

She should have taken Jane up on the offer of a sedative. Anything would be better than this emotional hell she was enduring.

In the end, she couldn't stand it any longer. Snapping a lamp back on, she threw back the sheet and swung her legs over onto the thick blue carpet. Levering herself up onto her feet, she forced herself to walk to the door and open it. Maybe Val had *something* she could take. Anything. A painkiller might do.

'Val?' she called out. Weakly at first, but then more loudly.

The door of his bedroom was wrenched open and there he stood, in nothing but those incredibly sexy silk pyjama pants, slung low on his hips. Her stomach lurched at the sight of his semi-naked body, then again at the thoughts which swiftly followed.

'What is it?' he bit out sharply. 'What's wrong?'

'I can't sleep,' she confessed, and he gave her an exasperated look.

'I did warn you, didn't I?'

'Do you have anything which might help me relax?'

He stared at her hard for a moment, and she wondered if he was reading her shameful mind. 'I might have something. Go back to bed. I'll bring it in to you.'

She was lying there stiffly under the sheet when he came in with what looked like a glass of water in his hand and nothing else.

'Drink this,' he ordered.

She drank, assuming some drug was dissolved in the water. 'What was it?' she asked as he took the empty glass and placed it down beside the lamp.

'Just water. I couldn't find anything. I'm not a tablet-taker. But it wasn't a tablet you were looking for when you called out to me, was it?'

'I don't know what you mean. Of course it was!'

'You might be able to fool yourself, Lucille, but you can't fool me. I could see it in your eyes when you looked at me. You want sex.'

Her heart quickened at his words, her lips parting.

'There's no shame in that,' he said matter-of-factly, taking her shoulders and pressing her back onto the pillow. 'So why deny it? Why deny yourself? You need to relax very badly, Lucille. A climax should do it. I can do that for you. You know I can. Just close your eyes, lie back, and let me...'

Lucille could feel her eyes closing, his shockingly seductive words stripping her of all will but to do exactly as he said.

After throwing back the sheet, he began by kissing her mouth, then her throat, slowly working his way down her body, his hands peeling the nightie from her tautly expectant body an inch or two at a time, gradually uncovering more bared skin for his lips to tease and torment on their way towards his ultimate goal.

If relaxing her was his intention, then it certainly wasn't his interim aim. He took for ever over her breasts, not moving on till her nipples were like glistening bullets, burning after being tugged at by his teeth, then sucked sweetly. Her stomach was like a rock by the time he licked his way over it, her spiralling desire having tightened her muscles till she felt as if she was stretched out on a rack. She could feel the wet heat of her arousal between her legs. Her thighs began quivering long before he reached them.

'Poor baby,' he murmured as he kissed the bruise on her hip, then again when he reached the one on her thigh.

She gasped when his mouth honed straight in on her clitoris. For by then she was screaming inside with need. There was no hope of hanging on for long after his tongue started flicking over that exquisitely sensitive mass of concentrated nerve-endings. When his lips actually closed around it, and sucked, she came with a rush and a strangled cry, her mind torn between delight and dismay.

'I'm sorry,' she sobbed, even as her flesh spasmed in the most blissful rapture. 'Sorry...'

'Don't be silly,' Val chided softly. 'There's nothing to be sorry about. I don't want anything for myself. This is for you, my darling. All for you...'

And, to her joy and astonishment, he bent his lips to her body once more.

* * *

'Sleep well?' was his first question when she finally had the courage to leave her room the following morning.

He was sitting at the breakfast bar on one of the stools, dressed all in black again. A mug of steaming coffee sat on his right, a newspaper was spread out before him. He'd shaved, ridding him of the stubble which he'd used to such tantalising effect on her the previous night.

Lucille didn't blush. She'd done all her blushing on first waking up. Now, she looked at him with curiosity, at this man who could give a woman so many mind-blowing climaxes without wanting anything for himself. Was that love? Or a ruthless route to a goal?

Lucille had to admit that it had been an incredible experience, and one which would enslave just about any woman.

'Very well, thanks to you,' she answered truthfully. 'And yourself?'

He shrugged, the hint of smile playing around his mouth. 'I've had better.'

'I feel a fraud not going to work,' she said. 'I feel marvellous.' Which, again, was true. Her body was at peace even if her mind wasn't as yet.

'Then come to the theatre with me,' he suggested. 'I won't be there all that long. A couple of hours at most. I've only got the two principals rehearsing today. I've given the rest of the cast the day off.'

'Why do you have to be there at all? Isn't that the director's job? My God, Val, you didn't fire him yesterday, did you?'

'No. He's come down with a gastric virus. That's why he was being such a pain. Hopefully it's one of those forty-eight-hour bugs and he'll be back on deck by tomorrow. But, to be honest, I'm glad to have a crack at sorting things out between Angela and Raoul without Nigel around. Something's going on there I don't like. A clash of egos, probably. But their most important dance—the tango, the climax to the show— is anything but inspiring at the moment. I'm going to give them both some come-hurry today, I can tell you. This show is going to be a smash hit, even if I have to turn into a bully-boy.'

'I can't imagine you ever being a bully-boy,' Lucille said thoughtfully.

Val smiled a wicked smile. 'That's because I've only showed you my good side so far.'

That was what Lucille was afraid of.

Still, she didn't mind the idea of seeing him bully this Angela around a bit. It would be her only chance of seeing 'Flame' in action on the stage. No way was she going to let Val persuade her to accompany him to the actual première on Friday night. After what had happened last night, it was pointless pretending she wasn't going to continue their affair. But their relationship was going to remain a very private romance for the time being.

'I'll come,' she said, 'if you promise me there won't be any photographers around.'

His smile faded. 'I don't invite the press to rehearsals,' he ground out. 'But if one happens to sneak in, then I'll introduce you as my cousin.'

'Sister would be better.'

'I don't *have* any sisters,' he snapped.

'Then invent one.'

CHAPTER THIRTEEN

LUCILLE sat in the shadows at the back of the theatre, watching proceedings from the safety of distance. An hour earlier she'd declined Val's offer to be introduced to Angela and Raoul, saying she'd rather not.

'Who do you expect me to say you are?' he'd demanded to know. 'I can't tell *them* you're my sister.'

'Don't tell them anything. I'll keep well in the background.'

He hadn't argued with her further, but he hadn't been pleased.

An hour had passed since then, and the two dancers were not pleasing Val, either. Their performance looked fine to Lucille, though she was no expert.

Raoul was a very attractive man, she noticed. Not as tall as Val, but lean and elegant, with the dark hair and eyes of most Latins, and a proud, rather sulky face.

As for Angela...

Lucille tried not to feel jealous or worried as she watched this girl whom Val had admitted to caring about. In the flesh, she was even more stunning than in her photograph. A vibrant, dark-eyed beauty, with full, sexy lips, lovely olive skin and the kind of lush, curvy figure which Val had already admitted to liking.

Neither dancer was in costume at the moment, though Angela *was* wearing a figure-revealing white leotard and tights. Lucille had no doubt that when she became 'Flame' for the show, her clothes would be as hot as her stage name suggested. Latin dancers were notorious for their scanty and very revealing clothes. Lucille's stomach tightened at the thought of Val lusting after this creature, despite having declared his love for *her*. Her jealousy was eased only by the thought that Angela had chosen the father, not the son.

But what would happen, she worried, if Angela ever changed her mind about that and switched her attentions to the son? How long would Val's so-called love for *her* last in the face of such a temptation?

'No, no, *no*!' Val exploded, snapping off the taped music. 'The tango is a sensual dance, for pity's sake, not some stiff set of prescribed steps, performed by robots. What in hell's wrong with you two? Put some passion in the damned thing. Now try it again, from the beginning.'

They both glowered at each other, then at Val, who glowered right back at them.

'I want you to look like you're burning for each other,' he ordered. 'It doesn't have to be real. Pretend. Act. A top dancer is a top actor. So act, damn you!'

When the music started up again, Lucille surreptitiously made her way a few rows closer, sitting down at one end and leaning her arms on the back of the seat in front of her. She wanted a closer view, to see if Val was being fair or just giving in to a bout of Latin temperament, for whatever reason.

This time, however, Lucille saw what Val was getting at. Although Raoul and Angela danced perfectly together, without putting a step wrong, there was a coldness to their movements and a lack of fire in their faces. They looked as if they despised each other.

Lucille hadn't noticed it before, from where she'd been sitting at the back, but she noticed it now.

Within a few bars, Val was on his feet again. 'Oh, for pity's sake!' he stormed, leaping onto the stage and pushing Raoul out of the way. 'You have no idea, do you? *This* is what I want.' And he yanked Angela into his arms. 'Now, dance the way you would,' he commanded, 'if you were really in love with your partner. Don't hold back. Give it all you've got.'

Lucille was both fascinated and appalled by what happened next.

As Val had just said, the tango was a sensual and passionate encounter, the artistic expression of a desire-filled man pursuing his woman, capturing and seducing her. Or so Lucille had always thought when she'd watched the dance before. Not that she'd ever seen it with live partners, only on television, or in the movies. It was, supposedly, an erotic experience for both dancers and onlookers.

Seeing Raoul and Angela dance it on stage hadn't ignited any heat within her.

Seeing Val and Angela perform the same dance, however, was a totally difference experience. At first, Lucille simply marvelled at Val's unexpected brilliance. Technically, he was every bit as good as Raoul. He'd said he liked to dance but she hadn't known he was this good. As Lucille watched him execute the difficult and dramatic steps, with amazing skill and assurance, she realised how apt his name was. Valentino—who'd been a great dancer before he'd become famous as a great lover.

Soon, however, Lucille ceased to wonder over the level of Val's talent, a fierce jealousy pushing all other feelings aside once she realised that what she was witnessing was no act. The passion in Val's face was too intense not to be real. The way he held his body—and Angela's—too achingly taut not to be the result of the most acute sexual tension.

Lucille could *feel* his tension. And his heat. It radiated from every pore of his stiffly held male body, stirring her despite the fact her lover no longer knew she was even there.

If I can feel all that from this distance, Lucille agonised, what must Angela be feeling, up there, in his arms?

Despair descended swiftly once Lucille saw the evidence of what Angela *was* feeling. Because she was no longer Angela. She was Flame. Flame who now had a partner who burned for her. She burned right back, her dark eyes never leaving his, even when her body was half turned away. Her head remained always fixed in Val's direction, galvanising him with a gaze so smouldering and seductive that Lucille's mouth went dry just looking at it. As she turned and twisted, Angela's body became the sultriest of weapons, taunting and tantalising, alternating a challenging resistance with moments of bone-melting surrender. When the dance called for Val to clasp her high to his chest, she lifted her leg and slowly rubbed her thigh down his as her feet slid back to the floor. By the time the dance ended, with Val dipping her back over his arm and looming over her arched body like the dominating male mate he obviously wanted to be, Lucille's stomach was churning.

She sighed a deeply shuddering sigh. God, what a fool I've been, hoping he might really be in love with me. Jane told me the truth. Only a woman of like mind and like nature would ever satisfy Val. You only had to look at them together to know how well matched they were, both in temperament and interest.

Lucille was sitting there, wretchedly wondering what she should do, when Raoul strode over and wrenched Angela out of Val's arms. He screamed something at them both in a language she didn't understand. Angela spat something back, then slapped him hard around the face. When Val tried to intervene, Raoul turned on him with another foreign stream of invective. And then it was on for young and old, insults flying back and forth, presumably.

Lucille might not understand a single word they were saying, but she could understand the tone and interpret the expressions on their faces. You didn't have to be a genius to see that this was another love triangle the man-hungry Angela was trying to engineer.

Lucille could not believe that a woman could be this manipulative, or this fickle. Did it turn her on to play one guy off against another?

In the end Raoul stormed off towards the stage exit and Angela threw herself, sobbing, into Val's arms.

Val didn't hesitate to cradle her head into that intimate little spot under his chin, stroking her dark glossy hair down her back and murmuring soothing endearments, this time in English.

'There, there,' he crooned. 'Don't take it to heart. He didn't mean it. I'm sure he still loves you. Quite a lot, I would imagine. No man gets that angry unless he's madly in love with the woman in question.'

Lucille almost groaned out loud, thinking of the first

day she'd met Val, and how angry he'd been over Angela sleeping with his father.

'You're wrong,' Angela sobbed. 'No one loves me any more. They all think I'm a whore. Max. Raoul. You.'

'Max doesn't think you're a whore. Max doesn't think like that. And I don't, either. But you have acted very badly,' he said gently. 'Sleeping with one man when it was really another you wanted. But I won't hold that against you. We all do stupid things when we're young.'

'You still love me?' she asked plaintively, with an upward sweep of her long dark lashes.

'I'll always love you, Angie, as you well know.'

Lucille's heart squeezed tight. He loved her. And he called her Angie. Not Angela. Angie...

'And I you, Valentino,' the girl returned warmly. 'You are the best of men. Much better than your father. I don't know why I went to bed with him. I must have been crazy. Raoul had just told me it was over between us and I was so hurt. I wanted to hurt him and I did. With Max.'

Val pulled away from her slightly, his expression surprised. 'You mean Max never seduced you?'

'No.' Angela slanted him a coy look. 'Any seducing was done by me. I can be a bad girl, Valentino. A very bad girl. Do you forgive me? I know how upset you were when you found me and your father in bed together.'

'Don't do it again.'

'I won't. I promise. And don't be mad at your father any more. It wasn't really his fault.'

Val's smile was wry. 'I guess resisting you in seduction mode would be a pretty impossible task for a man like Max. For just about any man, I would imagine.'

'You think so?'

'I think so.'

That was it! Lucille could not bear another moment. She was way beyond being some kind of maudlin victim who would let a man walk all over her and play her for a fool.

Launching herself up onto her feet, she marched up the aisle towards the stage, determined to put an end to this fiasco once and for all. Val's head jerked up from where it had been practically buried in Angela's hair, and he grimaced once he saw the expression on Lucille's face. He threw her an apologetic and pleading glance, as though all would be explained shortly. But it was far too late for that. Fury and outrage were already bubbling in her blood. Did he honestly think she would believe a word he said now?

'Do excuse me, Val,' she said coldly, 'but I have to go home. And I mean *home*, home, not your place.'

Angela's head snapped up from the sanctuary of Val's chest; she was clearly taken aback by the sight of Lucille standing there. No doubt the creature had been so self-absorbed all morning that she hadn't noticed her, sitting in the back stalls.

'Valentino?' Angela asked imperiously. 'Who *is* this woman?'

'This woman, my dear Angela,' Val said ruefully, 'is a woman who has no trust in the man who loves her.'

One of Lucille's eyebrows arched. If he imagined for one moment that he could convince her of some kind of platonic love for this girl, then he could think again. Actions spoke much more loudly than words. She'd seen him do the tango with his precious *Angie*. And she wouldn't forget it in a hurry!

Angela lifted startled eyes to the man whose arms were still around her. 'You *love* her?' she asked, clearly amazed.

'More than I'd ever thought possible.'

Angela squealed, rose up on tiptoe and began plastering kisses all over Val's face.

'Hey, stop that!' he protested, grabbing her hands and holding her away from him. 'You'll give Lucille the wrong idea again. She already thinks things between us are too close for comfort.'

Angela whirled to frown at Lucille. 'You think my Valentino would cheat on the woman he has waited a lifetime to fall in love with? What kind of fool are you? I don't think you deserve my brother's love,' she finished with an angry toss of her head.

'Your *brother*?' Lucille gasped.

'Half-brother, actually,' Val corrected when Lucille threw shocked eyes his way. 'Lucille didn't know we were related,' he directed back at Angela. 'You asked me not to say anything about our blood relationship, so I didn't.'

Angela pouted her ruby-red lips. 'That's no excuse. Even if you *weren't* my brother, she should have more faith in you. You are not like your father. Or stupid Raoul, for that matter, who never knows his own mind. You are good and kind and honest. So I still think she should apologise to you.'

Lucille stiffened at this. If anyone was going to do any apologising it should be Val, for lying to her about

Angela. And putting her through hell just now with the way he did the tango with his own sister.

Val saw the expression on her face and smiled a wry smile. 'Why don't you run along after Raoul and do some apologising yourself?' he told Angela. 'In your own inimitable way, of course.'

Angela's returning smile was quite wicked. 'You do realise that will be the end of rehearsing for the day?' she warned him.

'That's okay. Once you make up with him I'm sure Raoul will put some more passion into his dancing in future.'

'You could be right about that, brother.' Angela laughed as she sashayed saucily down the stage steps. 'Which is just as well, because that man can't act one little bit.'

'Hard to act when you're in love,' Val remarked, his eyes firmly on Lucille. 'The heart has a mind of its own.'

'Huh!' Angela snorted whilst Lucille continued to glare at Val. 'Most men don't know where their heart is. The only body part they can find is the one south of the border.' She was about to stalk past Lucille when she ground to a halt right in front of her. '*Most* men, I said,' she added, dark eyes flashing. 'Not my brother. He *does* have a heart. So take care not to hurt it, lady, or you'll have me to answer to. Believe me when I say I am not the soft touch my Valentino is. I come from slightly different stock. My father was a bullfighter!' With that, she tossed her head once more and marched off.

'Remind me never to cross your sister,' Lucille said drily once Angela was gone.

Val came slowly down the stage steps, his eyes never leaving hers. 'Or me,' he ground out. 'Now, stop looking at me like I've done anything wrong here. Angie's right. Your ignorance of my relationship with her is no excuse for your lack of faith. So what have you got to say for yourself, madam?' He halted right in front of her, his arms crossing, his brows beetling together.

'You dance very well,' Lucille remarked coolly, refusing to let Val intimidate her. 'You act very well too.'

'That was no act,' he grated out. 'Because I wasn't dancing with Angie. Not in my head. I was dancing with you, my lovely, foolish, faint-hearted Lucille.'

'Oh…' Guilt and delight consumed her, obliterating all her anger over his deception about his sister. 'Really?'

'Must I prove everything to you a thousand times?' He drew her forcefully into his arms. 'When are you just going to take my word for something?'

'Be fair, Val,' she argued back, struggling to stop him from holding her too close. She always had trouble thinking when he did that. 'Do you have any idea how threatening a woman like your sister would be to any relationship? She's so beautiful and sexy and…and…passionate. All the things I thought might tempt you. If you'd told me right from the start she was your sister, I might not have imagined such awful things. Or been so jealous. I'm sure Angela wouldn't have minded your telling me the truth in confidence.'

'Maybe I *wanted* you to be jealous,' he admitted, yanking her hard against him. 'Maybe I needed to see some evidence that you felt more for me than just lust.

But I didn't do it deliberately. Not in the beginning. Later, perhaps. I rather liked your reaction every time the fantastic Flame came up in our conversation. It gave me hope, rather than hurt. I've never had a woman not be proud to be by my side before. It's been a very difficult situation for me to bear.'

'Yes,' Lucille conceded at last, her voice and heart softening. 'Yes, I can see it must have been. I didn't mean to hurt you, Val. I was just so afraid of being hurt myself.'

'I know. And you probably had every reason to be. My past record with women didn't look good, did it? But I do love you, Lucille. Angie's right when she says I've waited a lifetime to fall in love. I have. I was beginning to think I never would. I sometimes wondered if I'd inherited my parents' fickleness in matters of the heart, because I never felt that special something people talk about. Till I met you...'

He bent his head and kissed her with a seductive mixture of tenderness and hunger. 'Tell me you love me,' he whispered urgently against her lips. '*Tell* me.'

'I...I love you,' she confessed shakily, and his arms tightened around her.

'Then don't keep me a secret any longer, my darling. I can't stand it. I want you by my side, openly. I want you to be proud of loving me. Come with me to the première on Friday night. Please, Lucille, don't say no. You have to rid yourself of this cynicism and start trusting again some time. Start by trusting *me*. I won't ever hurt you. I promise.'

Lucille's heart yearned to do what he wanted, even whilst her head still worried. But this time her heart won.

'All right,' she agreed on a quavery sigh.

Val groaned his satisfaction. 'I can't tell you how happy you've made me,' he murmured, and kissed her some more.

CHAPTER FOURTEEN

LUCILLE returned to her flat the following morning, still aglow from the night before. She would never have believed making love with Val could get any better, but it had. Telling Val that she loved him seemed to have increased her emotional *and* physical pleasure.

Smiling contentedly, she closed her front door and turned to see the light on her answering machine winking.

Her smile faded. Michele. It was sure to be Michele, wanting to make arrangements for this Friday night.

What on earth was she going to tell her? The truth, or more white lies?

No, she couldn't keep lying when she was going to be out in public with Val this Friday night. The media was sure to show interest in the new woman on his arm at such a well-publicised première. Photos of them both would be popping up in the weekend tabloids.

Lucille had already decided to go back to work this Thursday and Friday, because she could hardly have the whole week off and then be seen on Friday night, being escorted around Star City by one of Sydney's most eligible bachelors.

The same reasoning applied to Michele. She had to be told the truth.

Lucille dropped her overnight bag and walked over to press the 'rewind' and 'play' buttons on the answering machine. The first message, however, was from her mother.

'Mum, here. Just calling to see if you're all right. We haven't heard from you in ages. Please ring, Lucille. I've been a bit worried about you. Anyway, dear, I'm doing my Christmas shopping next week and wanted to see if there was anything special you'd like. Naturally we'll expect you home for Christmas Day. You can stay longer if you like. Though you never seem to want to...'

Lucille's heart caught at the sad note in her mother's voice. Guilt flooded her over not calling lately, or ever staying longer than was marginally polite. She was always so defensive where her family was concerned that she'd never stopped to think her standoffish behaviour might be hurtful.

She hadn't stopped to think she'd been hurting Val, either. Had she become one-eyed and selfish since leaving Roger? Suddenly she felt small and mean where her treatment of her family was concerned.

'...anyway, do give me a call this week, dear, when you have time. Bye for now.'

I'll make time, Mum, Lucille vowed. And I'll try to be a little more considerate of your feelings. I know I've been a disappointment to you, but I also know you do love me. You just don't always know how to show it. But then...I'm not much better.

'Lucille Jordan, where the hell are you?' the next voice on the answering machine demanded to know in frustrated tones. This time it *was* Michele. 'I called you at work and they said you were off sick. But you're not at home. My suspicion meter is running, I can tell you. Whatever, get better by Friday! Tyler's been able to get us these simply brilliant tickets to the opening night of that sexy South American dance show. Word is it's hot to trot. Plus the perfect place for you to wear that fab red dress. I told you it had the tango written all over it. Ring me as soon as you can. And no excuses now. You're going to that show with us and that's final!'

Lucille shook her head ruefully as she switched off the machine. She certainly *was* going to that show. She just wasn't going with Michele and Tyler

Fate seemed to have decided for Lucille. There was no way out now. Michele had to be told the truth, the whole truth, and nothing but the truth.

Lucille's stomach crunched down hard at the thought of her friend's possible reaction. Hopefully, Michele would be so pleased at her finding a man-friend that she might overlook being kept in the dark all this time. Still, Michele was sure to have a shot at her over Val being a reputed playboy. After all, she'd given Michele hell over Tyler's reputation with women.

Having resigned herself to some teasing, Lucille picked up the phone and dialed Michele's work number.

'Lucille! Thank God. Where have you been? And don't tell me you've been sick, because I won't believe you.'

'No, I wasn't sick. I was mugged. On Monday night.'

'Mugged! Oh, you poor thing. Are you all right? What happened?'

Lucille told her briefly what had happened.

Michele made sympathetic sounds. 'And there was

no one around to help you afterwards? How awful.
You should have called me straight away. I'd have
raced over and brought you home with me. You
shouldn't have been alone after something dreadful
like that happening to you.'

'Actually, I did call someone, Michele. And he took
me home to his place for the night.'

Michele's stark silence was telling. *'He?'* she
quizzed at last. 'Who, exactly, is *he*?'

Lucille took a deep breath. 'A man I've been seeing.
And please don't be angry with me, Michele. I met
him three weeks ago and I...I didn't want to say anything because I didn't think our affair would go anywhere.'

'Affair!' Michele squawked. 'You've been having
an affair with some man and you didn't tell me?'

'I'm sorry,' Lucille said sheepishly.

'She's sorry! You're certainly going to be if you
don't tell me all right here and now. Who is he?
How—and *when*—did you meet him? And don't even
think about leaving out a single solitary detail,
Lucille.'

Lucille winced. 'Well, I...er...met him three weeks
ago last Monday, through work. He's the man I found
the luxury flat in Darling Harbour for that day, remember?'

'Mr hard-to-satisfy Valentino. How could I forget?
I asked you about him and you said he'd be the last
man on earth you'd have a relationship with.'

'I hadn't been having a relationship with him then.
I'd only been having sex with him. And his name isn't
exactly Mr Valentino. It's Val Seymour. I'm sure

you've heard of him,' she added, then waited for the reaction.

'My God!' Michele exclaimed, then fell silent again.

'Is that all you have to say?'

'I'm speechless.'

'I know, I know. He's a playboy. But he's not as bad as he's reported to be. I thought he was in the beginning, and that's why I didn't want to tell you about him. But I don't think so any more. He's actually a very sweet man.'

'Is this Lucille Jordan, North Sydney's resident cynic, speaking here?'

'I'm trying hard not to be.' Lucille sighed. 'Look, Michele, you yourself said I had to get over my marriage and that I was to start living again.'

'You certainly took me at my word, didn't you? Having an affair with Val Seymour. Good Lord! He makes Tyler look tame! I still can't believe it.'

'You will when you see me with him at the première of *Takes Two to Tango* this Friday night,' Lucille said drily. 'He's the producer.'

'What? Oh, Lord, so he is. What a coincidence! But a fantastic one. I'm excited already. Ooh, I can't wait to see you with him, wearing *my* dress. Just wait till I tell Tyler. He'll be so pleased. He thinks you're a great girl and gets quite angry when I tell him you don't want anything to do with men any more. 'What a waste,' I think his most recent words were on the subject.'

'You...you don't think I'm being foolish, Michele?' she asked, doubt and fear returning with a rush.

'Don't be ridiculous! I couldn't have picked a better

man myself to crank up those cranky old hormones of yours.'

'Er…he's cranked up more than my hormones,' Lucille said gingerly. 'I've fallen in love with him.'

'Oh, dear, that's a worry. I thought you were just using him for sex and a bit of fun.'

'He…he says he's fallen in love with me too.'

'Oh well, that's all right, then.'

'You really think so, Michele?'

'Now why would a man like that say he loves you if he doesn't? Val Seymour could have any girl he wants without ever having to mention that particular four-letter word. Some sensible person told me the same thing about Tyler once, when I was having my doubts about him, and it made perfect sense to me. Now I'm saying it to you. Trust me on this, Lucille. And trust him. Because if you don't start trusting soon, you're going to be doomed to an eternity of misery.'

'I know you're right.'

'Of course I'm right. Can I be chief bridesmaid at your wedding?'

Lucille's stomach tightened. Why was it that Val's never mentioning marriage bothered her so much? As she'd told Jane, they'd hardly known each other long enough to consider such a serious commitment.

'It's a bit soon for marriage, don't you think?' Lucille said defensively.

'True. So when are you going to move in with him?'

'He asked me to, but I said no.'

'Good Lord, why? No, don't tell me why. I don't want to hear any more of your cynical views about men. Life is a gamble, Lucille, and so is love. If you don't play, you can never win.'

'I can never lose, either.'

'"'Tis better to have loved and lost Than never to have loved at all."'

Lucille laughed. 'You never give up, do you?'

'Not when my friend's happiness is at stake.'

Lucille was touched by her friend's words. And inspired as well. 'You're right,' she said firmly. 'It's time to take a chance.'

'Thatta girl!'

'I'll ring Val straight away. Tell him I'll move in this weekend.'

'Good idea.'

'Then I'm going to ring Mum and have a chat.'

'Did I hear right? Did you say you're going to ring your mother?'

'Yep.'

'This is too much. I'll have to hang up. There are only so many shocks a girl can take in one day.'

Lucille laughed. 'Sorry.'

'Don't be. They were all good news. But I really must go. See you Friday night. And don't forget to wear my red dress!'

Friday night came round all too quickly, with Lucille having a resurgence of nerves as she put the final touches to her appearance. She was at Val's place, and had been since shortly after she'd rung him on Wednesday and told him she'd like to live with him. He'd been such an eager beaver to get her here, dropping everything and racing over to help her move straight away.

Lucille hadn't been able to bring herself to abandon her flat entirely, that little niggle remaining that she might need somewhere to go back to in a hurry some time, if things didn't work out. Val didn't know she owned the place, so she hadn't volunteered that information, knowing it would only hurt him. He'd seemed genuinely thrilled with her decision and she hadn't wanted to dampen his enthusiasm. He was such a different Val from the angry man she'd first met. Full of the joy of living. He'd even made up with his father, and had spent considerable time on the phone the previous night telling him all about her.

Max—ever the superficial charmer—had waxed lyrical about her, saying he'd been very impressed on the two occasions he'd met her at Erica's place. *A class act*, was what he'd called her.

Her mother obviously didn't think so, however. Lucille had bravely told her about Val during her call home the other day, thinking that would be better than her mother finding out about him via the newspapers.

'I love him, Mum,' Lucille had relayed, hoping that would be enough. 'And he loves me.'

'That's all very well, dear,' her mother returned carefully. 'But men like that don't marry ordinary girls like you. If they marry at all, that is.'

Lucille flinched. Those sentiments were exactly what *she'd* first thought, practically word for word. She wondered if, down deep, she was a clone of her mother.

'I suppose you're sleeping with him,' her mother added before she could defend either herself or Val.

'Actually, I'm moving in with him today,' she replied in one of those bursts of rebellious defiance which always got her into trouble.

'Then he'll *never* marry you. Why buy a cow when you can get the milk for free?'

'Oh, Mum, that's so hopelessly old-fashioned.'

'Old-fashioned does not mean stupid, daughter. A lot of men would never marry if they had their way. Men like Val Seymour certainly have no need of it. They already have all the sex they want without giving their girfriends anything of lasting value except what's in their chequebooks. If this man truly loves you, he will want to marry you. He will also want your children. But he *won't* want to parade you around for people to talk about as little better than a tart.'

'I am *not* a tart.'

'No. You're not, Lucille Jordan. So don't do anything to make people think you are.'

'Mum,' she said, with the little patience she had left, 'I love this man and I'm going to live with him. Please try to understand and support me in this.'

'I just want you to be happy, Lucille,' was her mother's sad remark. 'I *know* you, daughter. You won't be happy without marriage and children. That's why I was so upset when you left Roger.'

'Roger was a pig, Mum. Not a prince.'

'And this Val is a prince?'

'*I* think so. And that's all that matters. Look, can I bring him home for Christmas, or not?'

'Of course you can. Just don't expect your father to be impressed with a man who won't marry his daughter.'

Lucille sighed just thinking about that call now. The trouble was, her mother was probably right. She wouldn't be truly happy without marriage and children. She also didn't like the thought of people speculating about her relationship with Val.

She wasn't much looking forward to Christmas, either. She'd rather not take Val home at all, if her family were going to look down their noses at him, but then he would start thinking *she* wasn't proud of him.

A tap on the bedroom door had her whirling round. 'No, don't come in,' she called out. 'I'm almost ready. I'll come out in a minute. I'm not late, am I?'

'No. Plenty of time. I just thought we'd open a bottle of champagne before the car arrives. Come out to the bar when you're ready.'

'Okay.'

Lucille had dressed in one of the guest-rooms, wanting to surprise Val with the finished product. The mirror showed Michele had been right about the red dress. It was seriously sexy and very glamorous-looking, now that she'd added the strappy gold sandals and gold drop earrings. She'd pulled her hair up at the sides but left the rest down to flow in a honey-blonde curtain over her largely bared back. Her make-up was just as dramatic, with loads of eye make-up and a bright red lipstick which matched the colour of the dress.

But it was her body which would perhaps stop Val in his tracks. With one of Femme Fatale's cleverly boned corsets, her lush figure had been shaped into a devilish hourglass, whittling her already small waist into a tiny circle whilst rounding her derrière and lifting her breasts to form an eye-popping cleavage.

Satisfied she looked as sensational as she'd hoped to look, Lucille sprayed some more Eternity perfume all over her body, picked up her swish gold evening purse and exited the room.

Her journey down the long rectangular-shaped living area was deliberately slow, her hips swaying as she undulated towards where Val was standing behind the bar, pouring champagne into a couple of glasses. His hand froze, mid-air, once he spotted her, his eyes telling her all she needed to know.

'Wow,' he said in awed tones when she drew near. 'That is *some* dress. And some woman in it.'

'Thank you,' she said coolly, even though her heart was pounding. Partly from the way he was looking at her, but mostly from his own dashing appearance. Most men looked good in a black tie outfit, but Val took her breath away.

'You look very handsome,' she told him.

'And you'll outshine every woman there tonight.'

'Michele said it had the tango written all over it.'

'She's right.' He put the bottle down and came round from behind the bar, stretching out his right hand as he approached, his head held high, his body in instant tango mode. 'Shall we?'

'But I don't know the tango.'

'Can you dance at all?'

'Yes. I'm quite good.'

'No trouble, then. I'll lead. You follow. Just watch my eyes, and trust me.'

Lucille laughed. 'Don't you mean watch my feet?'

'Never do that with the tango. Always look into your partner's eyes.'

'What about music?'

'I'll supply that,' he said, and began to hum the famous tango number from *Phantom of the Opera*.

His left hand landed firmly in the small of her back, his right clasping hers away from their bodies.

Lucille had no idea how he managed it, or how she managed it. But dance the tango they did. Or a version of it. Their own private and personal version, full of a passion and intimacy which stunned her. Not even when Val had been making love to her had she felt such a complete bonding with him.

It wasn't till he dipped her back over his arm in a dashing finale that she realised it was all in the eyes.

It was said eyes were the windows to the soul, and they were, once all defences were down and the true soul was allowed to shine through. His eyes told her of the depth of his love for her. She could only hope hers were telling him the same.

'It's no good,' he groaned, and wrenched her back upright. 'It can't wait. I have to do it now.'

Abandoning her abruptly, he stalked off towards his bedroom, leaving Lucille to stare after him, her heart racing madly. Where was Val going? And what did he have to do now?

He was gone for less than twenty seconds, returning with rapid strides to bring him back to where she hadn't moved a muscle. When he dropped down onto his knee in front of her, she gasped. When he flipped open a small green velvet box he'd had hidden in his hand, her stomach squeezed tight.

A huge emerald and diamond ring sparkled up at her.

'I know this is premature,' he said, his expression almost anguished. 'I know I'm risking rejection. But I can't stand it any more, Lucille. I love you so much and I know you love me. Say you'll marry me. The wedding doesn't have to be too soon, if you need time to be sure. I'll wait. I'll wait for you for ever.'

Lucille could not believe the joy which burst into her heart with his wonderful words. Tears filled her eyes.

'Oh, Val...'

'I hope they're tears of happiness I'm seeing,' he said thickly. 'I hope that means yes.'

'It means yes,' she managed huskily, her whole being choked up with emotion.

He jumped to his feet, his face astounded but joyous. 'Yes!' he cried. 'My God, she said yes!'

'Yes,' she agreed, smiling at his shocked delight.

'And you like the ring I picked out? I thought it matched your lovely green eyes.'

'It's magnificent. I hope it fits.'

'I hope so too. I studied your finger for ages and it seemed about the same size as Angie's. So I took her along for sizing.' He plucked the ring out of its velvet nest and slipped it on, sighing with pleasure when it fitted perfectly. He grinned into Lucille's equally delighted face. 'By the way, Angie said to tell you that if you didn't say yes, you'd have her to answer to.'

Lucille rolled her eyes. 'That sister of yours is terrifying, Val. Poor Raoul.'

'Poor Raoul is getting plenty of what he likes best. And his performance tonight will reflect that. But I doubt it's a case of true love. Angie's just like Mamá. She gets carried away with the heat of the moment, but then grows bored. She's not interested in ever getting married, or having children. All she wants is her career.'

'And you, Val?' Lucille asked, now that he'd given

her the opening. 'Are you interested in having children?'

He groaned. 'I was worried you might ask me that. Now I'm terrified what answer to give you. Let me just say I want whatever you want. I know you were traumatised by losing your baby. I will understand if you never want to risk anything like that again.'

'Val,' Lucille said firmly. '*Do* you want children?'

'Yes. Oh, God, yes. I would *adore* having babies with you.'

'Babies! I'm nearly thirty-one, you know.'

'Which is why we should get married soon, don't you think? There's no time to waste.'

'Val Seymour, you are the most wonderful man in the whole wide world and I love you to pieces. But I'm not going to rush into anything. I want at least six months of sex and sin before settling down to married life and having a baby. But after that it's all systems go for a couple of new Seymour Productions.'

'I think we should drink to that.' He raced over to the bar and brought back the glasses of bubbly. 'To my lovely fiancée,' he toasted, clinking her glass with his, 'and the future mother of at least two little Seymours.'

'And to my handsome fiancé,' Lucille countered. 'The man who restored my faith in love, and in men. He's going to make a fantastic father, almost as good as he is a lover.'

His eyes melted all over her. 'I hope you'll still think that in thirty years' time…'

'Do you think we'll still be doing it in thirty years?' she mocked.

Val drew himself up straight and tall. 'Speak for yourself. I have very virile genes.'

Lucille thought of Max, still going strong at sixty, and with no sign of flagging. 'Too true. Just make sure you keep your virility for none other than yours truly.'

'I will. I promise.'

'If you don't,' she warned, 'you might find yourself minus part of your anatomy.'

'You'll have to get in quick, then. Because if you said yes to marrying me, Angie also threatened to castrate me if I was ever unfaithful to you.'

Lucille laughed. 'Now, *that* I would believe.'

The phone began to ring.

'That'll be the car,' Val said. 'Time to go...'

It was less than a minute's drive to the theatre from Val's apartment block, but they could hardly have arrived on foot in their finery. Hence the hire car.

The press photographers were certainly there when the white limousine pulled up at the grand steps leading up to the Casino and the theatre. Another limousine was pulling away just ahead of them, having deposited a couple, both of whom Lucille recognised. Max, suavely handsome in a white dinner jacket, escorting Erica, looking smug and sleek in beaded black.

Lucille's boss didn't bat an eyelid on seeing Lucille alight with Val, making Lucille conclude Max had already told her of his son's new lady-friend.

Erica sidled over close to Lucille as soon as they'd reached the top of the steps and the photographers had left them to race back down to the street below. A famous American movie producer and his model mistress had just arrived, thank heavens.

'I see you got over your aversion to playboys,

Lucille,' Erica murmured drily as they made their way into the foyer of the theatre.

'Not at all,' Lucille replied with cool aplomb. 'My fiancé has taken himself out of the playboy scene,' she added, waving her ring under her boss's nose.

'My God!' Erica exclaimed. 'Max didn't tell me about that. Max! Stop talking shop to Val and take a gander at this rock your son has given my best employee. Oh, darn, does that mean you'll be resigning soon to go flitting around the world with him?'

'Could be,' Lucille said noncommittally. She hadn't discussed the details of their future with Val yet, but she wouldn't mind. She'd always wanted to travel.

Max came over, beaming. 'Val was just telling me about that. Congratulations, Lucille. You've got yourself one great guy, even if I say so myself. Not that he hasn't snared himself one very lovely lady. Yes, very lovely indeed.'

'Eyes off, Dad,' Val ordered as he slid an arm easily around Lucille's tiny waist. 'She's all mine. Got a sec, darling? I need to talk to you alone for a minute.'

Lucille frowned as Val drew her aside. She tried not to panic, but her happiness was so new and so amazing that she still feared something might spoil it.

'What is it? What's wrong?'

'There's a man standing over there at the bar who's staring at you like he's seen a ghost. Do you know him?'

Lucille glanced over her shoulder to find Michele's gorgeous husband standing there with a cocktail frozen in his hand, his beautiful blue eyes glued to her.

Lucille smiled a relieved smile. For a second there she'd been worried it might be Roger. She never wanted to see that pig ever again. 'Oh, that's just Tyler,' she said off-handedly. 'Michele's husband.'

'Thank God for that,' Val muttered. 'He's too bloody good-looking to be competition. For a second there I thought I was going to have to fight a duel.'

'Don't be silly, darling,' Lucille chided. 'Men don't fight duels any more. Come over and I'll introduce you.'

She did just that, before asking Tyler where Michele was.

'Gone to the ladies' room. She's worried her dress might be too tight since she put on a bit of weight. Speaking of dresses, is that the one Michele picked out?'

'Yes. Do you like it?'

'Do I have red blood running through my veins?' he joked. 'Yes. I like it. You look fantastic, Lucille. You're a lucky man, Val. This girl is not only beautiful. She's darn choosy.'

'So I've gathered. Which makes me doubly proud that she's chosen me to marry.' Val's arm was around her again, drawing her close by his side.

Lucille knew he was staking out his territory with her, but she didn't mind. A certain amount of jealousy and possessiveness in a man was understandable, especially when they were in the company of another highly attractive and high-powered man.

'You're *engaged*?' Tyler sounded startled.

'Since a half-hour ago tonight,' Val announced.

'My God, Michele's going to flip. When's the wedding?'

'As soon as Lucille gives me the go-ahead.'

'Pin her down to a definite date, man,' Tyler advised. 'Girls these days are the very devil when it comes to commitment.'

'I know what you mean,' Val agreed ruefully.

'What?' Lucille exclaimed. 'Are you serious, you two?' She started shaking her head. 'Michele is not going to believe this.'

'Believe what?' the girl herself said as she materialised by Lucille's side. She was wearing the candy-pink number that looked as if it was sown on.

'Tyler and Val think we women have a problem with commitment these days. This is Michele, by the way, Val. My best friend. And, Michele, this is Val. My fiancé,' she added coyly, holding up her left hand and wriggling her fingers Michele's nose.

Michele screamed, and every head in the place jerked round to stare at them. Michele just shrugged. 'They're getting married,' she told all the curious on-lookers. 'I was just pleased, that's all.'

Everyone smiled, then went back to their own business.

'So when's the wedding?' she asked Lucille.

Lucille looked at Val, who looked expectantly back at Lucille.

'Easter,' Lucille decided with a resigned sigh. 'How about Easter?'

'Easter's fine,' Val said.

'No, it's not,' Michele wailed. 'I'll be as big as a bus by then. I'll be the fattest, ugliest matron of honour who ever walked the face of the earth.'

'Nonsense,' Tyler contradicted. 'You could never be anything but beautiful.'

'We'll find you the perfect dress,' Lucille promised. 'Something floaty and feminine.'

'Could it be low-cut at the front?' Michele asked, the sparkle back in her eyes. 'I just realised my boobs are going to be enormous by then too. I might as well flaunt them while I have them.'

'You can have whatever you like.'

Michele grinned. 'Okay, then, you have my approval to get married at Easter.'

Lucille smiled at her friend. Then smiled at Val. He smiled back and her heart overflowed with happiness. What a wonderful night, she thought. All that was needed to complete her happiness was for the show to be a big hit.

'Time to go in, everyone,' Max called over. 'The warning bell's gone.'

Lucille felt the instant stiffening in Val's body where she was holding his arm. He was obviously worried about the show. And why wouldn't he be? He'd worked so hard. And he cared so much. Too much, perhaps. There again, he wouldn't be the man he was if he wasn't passionate about what he did.

She squeezed his arm, and he smiled down at her. 'I'll be fine,' he said soothingly. 'Soon. It's only a show, after all. What really matters is you and me.'

'It would be nice to have a hit, all the same.'

'Yes,' he admitted with a nod of his handsome head. 'Yes, it would.'

The show was a *big* hit. But not as big a hit as Val was on Christmas Day. Her father was most impressed, now that they were safely engaged, with the wedding on the horizon. Her sisters thought Val was a dreamboat. Her nieces and nephews just adored him, because he'd bought them fantastic gifts. Even her two stodgy brothers-in-law seemed to get along with him. Still, Val could be a charmer when he put his mind to it.

Lucille's mother took her time coming round, however, saying nothing much for ages. But late in the afternoon, well after Christmas dinner was over, she drew her youngest daughter aside into a private corner of the house.

'I just wanted to say,' she said, 'that I think your Val is quite wonderful, and I think he's going to make you very happy. I've been watching him with you, listening to the way he speaks to you, seeing the way he touches you, the way he simply adores you. Yes, he *is* a prince, Lucille, whereas that Roger was just a frog pretending to be a prince. I can see the difference now, and I want to say how sorry I am that I didn't see it before. But it's not too late, is it, for a mother to apologise? I only ever wanted you to be happy, you know, Lucille.'

Lucille burst into tears and threw herself into her mother's arms. 'And I only ever wanted you to be proud of me,' she cried.

'But I've always been proud of you,' her mother said, stroking her hair. 'Always. How could I not have been? You're such a beautiful girl. And so bright. Ah yes, you worried me a lot. You wanted so much out of life. And you never wanted to wait for anything. I was concerned you would always be doomed to disappointment. But you've come up trumps this time, love. Val's going to make a wonderful father, so don't waste any time having that family he keeps talking about. You're not getting any younger, you know.'

'But we're not getting married till Easter,' Lucille protested.

'Since when did a little thing like that stop a rebel like you?'

'Mum, I'm shocked.'

'Really? Haven't you ever realised that your oldest sister, Katie, was born five months after your dad and I were married?'

'Golly, no! I didn't know that.'

'It wasn't all your father's doing, either.'

'Heavens!'

'You might find you're more like your old mum than you realise,' Mrs Jordan said, grey eyes twinkling. 'Why do you think I tried to be so strict with you when you were a teenager? Because I knew you were a chip off the old block. Now, go and take your man home to bed. And throw away those condom things. Men don't like them much, anyway.'

For the first time in her life Lucille did what her mother told her. When she married Val the following Easter, the whole female side of the official wedding party was pregnant. Michele was almost seven months—a girl, according to the ultrasound. Lucille was just over three. Jane was a month gone. And Angie an astonishing six weeks.

It seemed Raoul hadn't been prepared for his partner's spontaneous passion one night straight after the show, the fire ignited by his tango ending in an unexpected conception.

Surprisingly, Angie didn't mind. Raoul would make a lovely baby, she decided. But a simply dreadful husband. And he agreed with her. So no marriage was in sight. Her plan was to hire help and go back to dancing after the baby was born.

Val had thrown up his hands in despair at this, saying she was just like their mother. But he loved his sister all the same.

Val was a man with a lot of love to give, Lucille was to find, especially for his firstborn—a son, Christian, the apple of his eye. Till his daughter, Isabel, came along, that was. But neither child ever took away from the love he held for his wife. She was everything to him, that special woman he'd waited thirty-three years to meet and fall in love with.

And he never let her forget it.

HARLEQUIN Presents

Passion™

Looking for stories that **sizzle**?

Wanting a read that has a little extra **spice**?

Harlequin Presents® is thrilled to bring you romances that turn up the **heat**!

Every other month there'll be a
PRESENTS PASSION™
book by one of your favorite authors.

Don't miss
THE SPANISH HUSBAND
by **Michelle Reid**

On sale December, Harlequin Presents® #2145

Pick up a **PRESENTS PASSION™**—
where **seduction** is guaranteed!

Available wherever Harlequin books are sold.

HARLEQUIN®
Makes any time special ™

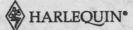

You're not going to believe this offer!

In October and November 2000, buy any two Harlequin or Silhouette books and save $10.00 off future purchases, or buy any three and save $20.00 off future purchases!

Just fill out this form and attach 2 proofs of purchase (cash register receipts) from October and November 2000 books and Harlequin will send you a coupon booklet worth a total savings of $10.00 off future purchases of Harlequin and Silhouette books in 2001. Send us 3 proofs of purchase and we will send you a coupon booklet worth a total savings of $20.00 off future purchases.

Saving money has never been this easy.

I accept your offer! Please send me a coupon booklet:

Name: _____

Address: _____ City: _____

State/Prov.: _____ Zip/Postal Code: _____

Optional Survey!

In a typical month, how many Harlequin or Silhouette books would you buy <u>new</u> at retail stores?

☐ Less than 1　　☐ 1　　☐ 2　　☐ 3 to 4　　☐ 5+

Which of the following statements best describes how you <u>buy</u> Harlequin or Silhouette books? Choose one answer only that <u>best</u> describes you.

☐ I am a regular buyer and reader
☐ I am a regular reader but buy only occasionally
☐ I only buy and read for specific times of the year, e.g. vacations
☐ I subscribe through Reader Service but also buy at retail stores
☐ I mainly borrow and buy only occasionally
☐ I am an occasional buyer and reader

Which of the following statements best describes how you <u>choose</u> the Harlequin and Silhouette series books you buy <u>new</u> at retail stores? By "series," we mean books within a particular line, such as *Harlequin PRESENTS* or *Silhouette SPECIAL EDITION.* Choose one answer only that <u>best</u> describes you.

☐ I only buy books from my favorite series
☐ I generally buy books from my favorite series but also buy
　 books from other series on occasion
☐ I buy some books from my favorite series but also buy from
　 many other series regularly
☐ I buy all types of books depending on my mood and what
　 I find interesting and have no favorite series

Please send this form, along with your cash register receipts as proofs of purchase, to:
In the U.S.: Harlequin Books, P.O. Box 9057, Buffalo, NY 14269
In Canada: Harlequin Books, P.O. Box 622, Fort Erie, Ontario L2A 5X3
(Allow 4-6 weeks for delivery) Offer expires December 31, 2000.

PHQ4002

Romance is just one click away!

online book serials

- *Exclusive* to our web site, get caught up in both the daily and weekly online installments of new romance stories.
- Try the Writing Round Robin. Contribute a chapter to a story created by our members. Plus, winners will get prizes.

romantic travel

- Want to know where the best place to kiss in New York City is, or which restaurant in Los Angeles is the most romantic? Check out our Romantic Hot Spots for the scoop.
- Share your travel tips and stories with us on the romantic travel message boards.

romantic reading library

- Relax as you read our collection of Romantic Poetry.
- Take a peek at the Top 10 Most Romantic Lines!

Visit us online at

www.eHarlequin.com
on Women.com Networks

CELEBRATE VALENTINE'S DAY WITH HARLEQUIN®'S LATEST TITLE—

Stolen Memories

Available in trade-size format, this collector's edition contains three full-length novels by *New York Times* bestselling authors Jayne Ann Krentz and Tess Gerritsen, along with national bestselling author Stella Cameron.

TEST OF TIME by **Jayne Ann Krentz**—

He married for the best reason.... She married for the only reason.... Did they stand a chance at making the only reason the real reason to share a lifetime?

THIEF OF HEARTS by **Tess Gerritsen**—

Their distrust of each other was only as strong as their desire. And Jordan began to fear that Diana was more than just a thief of hearts.

MOONTIDE by **Stella Cameron**—

For Andrew, Greer's return is a miracle. It had broken his heart to let her go. Now fate has brought them back together. And he won't lose her again...

Make this Valentine's Day one to remember!

Look for this exciting collector's edition
on sale January 2001 at your favorite retail outlet.

HARLEQUIN®
Makes any time special ™

Visit us at www.eHarlequin.com

PHSM